MW01600657

Pabulum Nation

By

Nova Schurdevin

This is a work of fiction.
Names, characters,

organizations, places, events,
and incidents are.

either products of the
author's imagination or are

used fictitiously. Any
resemblance to actual

persons, living or dead, or
actual events are purely
coincidental.

PabuLum Nation

by

Rachel Schurdevir

1

The year 2821, an archaeological dig had discovered the remains of what seemed to be a small town. The professor ushered his students into the dig site.

"You see kids, this was the year, 2023."

"Yep, carbon readings confirmed, this was the year that the people of the past ruined the planet."

"As primitive as it seems, they mined the earth for these containers."

Mr. Norman held up a clear shaped bottle with words that were too faded to read. "This is plastic."

"The early unevolved species of the planet would mine fossil fuels from the earth called oil and gasoline and use their by-products to sustain their economy."

"Of course, that would ultimately be their downfall."

"Causing the Great Shift... We can all be so fortunate to not have had to grow up in such a barbaric time in history and would not teach it." He wiped his brow and continued digging.

"We have here fossil evidence of the types of animals that were present during that era. This one is an owl. He pointed.

"You see kids", muffled. He popped his head up.

"Before these people began to become more like our society, they would wipe out over 75% of the earth's wildlife. They would kill off most of the oceans and fish. Geezz, what a mess."   The professor was glowing with absolute excitement. No one had seen artifacts like this in decades. Our world had changed so much since those dark years and most scholars laughed at the ridiculous behavior of our ancestors as a time of shame and would not teach it. "Professor Norman, why do you think early humans were consumed with this plastic consumption, and what did you call, ahh, Fossil fuel?"

"Well kids, you see they had built a society based on traditions passed down from hundreds and even thousands of years. These traditions once meant something to the ancestors and creators of the social norms, but once complacent on those ideologies; they lost focus of the harmony of the Great Divine Architect in the meaning of what even earlier predecessors to this era once believed."

"We all know that we are all an equally balanced ecosystem in harmony and exact balance with the Great Architect. These poor fools, well, their primitive religions lost meaning much like even earlier Greek mythology. So, their worship came in the form of greed and money."

"You see children, cultures had been creating and destroying themselves over, and, over again in history and this era would be no different. Consumed with consumption and money, we see the direct clash between the modern computing future, harmonious natural balance, and the traditions of the past. It would ultimately lead to their destruction."

"Mr. Norman, what caused the Great Shift?"

"Well, I guess, I would say. When the people finally woke up. The Great Awakening. I imagine if our society were drowning in its own trash and riddled with disease and consumption…...well we would probably wake up too."

"Mountains of trash kids, as we will see in this dig. I can almost promise you. Wherever we find human structures of this era we find lots of trash."

Mr. Norman was almost head deep in the dirt at this point throwing what looked like crushed frozen paint.

The bottles were brightly colored and marketed with logos of business long past.

"Look kids this one says Cellog's."

"Check it out.

The lion says…. That's Ggggggreat."

"A lion kids, there are only 300 in existence after the repopulation project."

"I saw one once with my dad as a kid". Mr. Norman reflected, scratching his head.

I picked up the box and read. What were these words? I had never seen such things.

"Mr. Norman, what is this?". He popped his head up out of the hole again. Laughing, he explained.

"This plastic... These by-products of chemicals, well kids, they ate them... in their food."

"What, No way, Gross...."

"Right, I know." He laughed.

"This culture kids," He leaned up on his elbows and faced the class. "You got to understand, they killed the planet with chemicals and fossil fuels."

"Took your grandfather's 100 years to fix half the mess they created."

"Tonight's homework read 'How the Divine Architect Fixed Their Mess.' Chapters 1-5. We will discuss this more tomorrow."

"I've got to see what else is buried here."

"Good-bye kids. Read." And back in the hole, he went.

You didn't have to tell me twice, let's go. I grabbed my stuff and out the door I went. Squeezing past everyone as fast as I could. The town festival was tonight, and I wasn't missing it for a minute. Our Town has been nominated the most Balanced town in Pabulum Nation and there were going to be people from all over the world coming to see the progress we had made in becoming fully optimized and waste-free. My parents would be so happy. They had established the most current algorithms, and although away on a humanitarian mission to repopulate the rainforest, their hard work has paid off. I worked at the local apothecary, so it was time to get the store up and ready for our guests.

Slamming the door behind me, I see the rest of my family scattering about preparing for the feast.

"Nova, are these tomatoes divine our what?" Shuttered Avus, grandfather

"We harvested these today just for the feast. I can't wait for Elisi, grandmother, to fix up some of her famous Tomato pies."

"Yummy!" Babbled Robyn, my little sister.

Oh, the thought of those pies I could not wait till tonight.

In Pabulum Nation each family grew together, of course, there were some family members who left off to see the world, join the Nation's Guard, or study abroad but growing is what saved the world, so it was each family's shift per se to serve the Great Architect in his divine plan. To be in one with the sacred geometry, that which all is made. The fabric of the multiverse is seamlessly perfect in all its imperfections, the map to evolution, and the planning of the harvests for generations to come.

The sun told us the time, the moon, the day, and the stars the month but the forests were our lungs, the oceans, and rivers our blood, and the earth our body. How we treated ourselves reflected how we treated our Mother Earth, our planet.

The gardens were indeed sublime, as I left the house to help pick. I walked out the backdoor to the patio and cast my eyes upon the glistening of brightly colored vegetables popping out amongst the green. Red, yellow, orange peppers, Tomatoes of so many colors and melons. Oh, how awesome this feast would be. I only hoped that the guests would be as pleased with our town's mission as we were. We had been nominated a few years back but when the Town's computing system got a glitch it set us back. We were ready to win that prize this year for sure. Our neighbor's son and his wife were quantum engineers and together with all the neighbors they had developed the town's network. This year's system had become so optimized that each person got rewarded for minimizing the town's carbon imprint. We were ready for sure. With zero waste and the optimization carbon award, we would create enough tourism to put us on the Nation's top 10 for most harmonious destinations.

A prize we were fully determined to win. I daydreamed of being handed my hard-earned reward, as I picked. Filling my basket to the top. Suddenly I stopped the basket full and ran into the house.

"But what should I wear, Elisi?"

"Nova this always seems to be the dilemma for every young woman welcoming new people into her hometown," she giggled.

"Wear a dress I suppose, a pretty one." she said.

I had just purchased the most beautiful silk dress. I hoped it would be here in time. My new silk dress, my hemp sandals, and of course, a flower for my hair.

My outfit was complete. I kissed Elisi on the cheek, hugged her neck, patted Robyn on the head and off I scampered smiling to seize the day.

It was a most beautiful day, the insects singing, the birds chirping, and little children laughing throughout the street. I walked and remembered what Mr. Norman was saying about the past. How could they kill off all the animals, bees, and insects?

How could they not want to be part of the harmony of the Multiverse?

Killing animals eating and consuming chemicals and plastics.

Drowning in the trash?

Who or what were these people?

Seemed like the ancient fables and myths of human sacrifices in the archives of history the scholars tell stories of. Greed...hhmmm, was a word that Mr. Norman said. It was not a familiar word; we knew no greed. Everyone in Pabulum nation shared. We all had enough. We were all in harmony with exactly all we needed to make life balanced and happy. What more, plastic stuff, could one need? It seemed so silly to want and want things to throw in the trash. What a weird society they were. It made no sense to me at all. I pondered, not wanting to think of such a harsh time for humanity and just then a butterfly landed on the flower in my hair. All seemed so good in the world. Thank goodness our people learned and studied the ways of our Mother Earth. Most children were raised with the teaching of the Scholars. The ways of the Divine Architect were to be memorized by first grade as a source to all sacred geometry. Each town commits to a small part of the whole, with each province owning its mission to optimize the carbon imprint and awarded for their harmony with nature. It was a great honor for our town to be nominated and each citizen worked together as a team to reach this year's goals. We were so proud to have reached Balance. The term was coined as the quest for town elegance. Harmony was when you reached equivalence. The measurement for which we strive. Every member in town works towards an egalitarian environment. Food is grown in balance with trees; grown to set apart from the transportation system, keeping the planet cool. Hemp and bamboo forests are grown to protect trees and the ocean and rivers are fished as they are studied and replenished to the exact balance of our community. Animals are cared for and harvested only with symmetry to healthy herd populations, allowed to roam free to be part of our ecosystem. Births are directly in harmony with deaths to maintain healthy population standards, thus always keeping in balance. Honoring the Sacred Geometry of the Divine Architect with our science as to achieving balance in nature and our community. It was our way and we loved and cared for our communities as one would care for a garden.

The Gardens of Greta are the province's crowning jewel. These gardens were the standard to which all cities strived to reach Balance. Over 150 acres of fruit trees and bushes, flowers, and beehives; the perfect unison with sculptures and ponds. Holograms tell of the leaders of Pabulum Nation and their quest to spread the teaching of the Divine Architect. The gardens were immensely beautiful. A central area dedicated to religions and spirituality with teachings of the past.

This year's judges would be the caretakers of the Gardens of Greta. They were accomplished scholars and botanists with teams of computer scientists that ran algorithms to the exact optimization of each town to see which of the 4 towns nominated would win. We all had worked so hard this year, and then my thoughts were suddenly interrupted.

"Booooo", startled. I laughed.

"Amida, where have you been?"

"I've been looking everywhere for you." A handsome Asian young man appeared from behind an apple tree laughing.

"You know I had to help my mom. She is crazy, cleaning and preparing for the festival." He laughed again crouching down to readjust his shoe.

"Did you hear about Mr. Norman's archaeological find?"

"Yes, I was there, he is astonished by the number of things he has found."

"Come on Nova, let's go check it out." Said Amida.

"We're not allowed to go down there without Mr. Norman." I replied.

"Besides, did you see the things they were pulling out of there?"

"The scientists were putting them in boxes to keep the poisons from leaking out. There is no way I am going down there." I stated.

"But Haalima said she saw them carrying books. I know you have been interested in ancient books, forever."

"Can you imagine finding some insight into the Great shift?"

"I know it's what you wrote your midterm and most of your final about."

"What if there are books that tell what happened?"

"I don't know Amida. It just seems so risky. Let's think about it on our way to the mail center. I'm curious about ancient books but I'm waiting for a dress, and it must be here before tonight. The tracker says it's at the mail center, so I'm hoping to get it before the drones are sent out to deliver it."

"Okay, Nova, I'll walk with you." He remarked.

"Hey Nova, Amida…. hey, wait up." Haalima shouted as she ran to catch up. Dropping her book and picking it back up again.

"Hey, wait for me. I'm trying to show you something."

"Hurry, Haalima. I'm trying to get to the mail center before the drones are sent out." I shouted.

"I'm coming." she replied, tripping over her satchel.

"OMDA Nova," panting. She ran up to us. "Oh my, Divine Architect you must see this book. I took it from the dig site. I can't believe the images."

"Look, Amida," with a little tension between them. She held up a weird-looking book. It was slim and larger than the books I had seen before and, on the cover, it said 'Time Magazine Nov. 2020'.

What was it about? I wondered?

The pages were dusty, and the cover was ripped but still intact.

On the cover of blue and red was a woman wearing a cloth over her face. The letters bold Said 'Vote'. And it was a special edition. The colors seem symbolic to the message it was trying to create. These years in time 2020 had been shrouded in mystery. Most of the printed books had been destroyed in the great clean-up. Radioactive and poisoned a lot of the history of the planet was lost. Questions like how they let it get so bad and why were kind of skipped over or vaguely answered by professors as the Dark Times and the Great Shift and Great Awakening which precluded the founding of Pabulum Nation. But that's really all the explanation they gave. The Great Architect had taught and showed the Nation's people the ways of Harmony and Balance, so that we should become one with Mother Earth and our people, but how the ancients destroyed the planet no one ever really spoke of.

"Just a stain on the creation of man." Mr. Norman always said.

All we were taught was not to be like that era. Much like the stories of the archives. The religions of myths and the fragments of what computing systems could be salvaged. It seemed that while earlier time periods were still interested in learning and balance with their planet, this era was consumed with war, consumption, greed, and chemicals. Our elders would simply not teach it. We had heard of the ancient Greek and Roman Gods, the Jews, Jesus, Buddha, And Muhammad their stories seemed ancient and sweet to heal and preserve. But, what of this era? The information was lost. Blamed on the sickness and greed that all seemed to go hand in hand.

As I flipped through the ragged pages, I read advertisements for chemicals to make you well or feed you. It was weird as I read the ads.

"Look, Haalima, this product makes you better it said but the very next page listed an entire page of things that could happen to you if you took it." Laughing and laughing.

 "Anal leakage, hahahaha, heart attack, seizures, oh my goodness this is hilarious."

"Well, the people looked happy." Said Amida.

The people in the pictures were smiling and laughing as if all was well.

"But why do you think they needed this stuff if they were so happy?" Asked Haalima.

"I think if I were going to have a heart attack, I'd just eat better foods." Interjected Amida.

"Like Doctor Jarreau always says prevention is in how you eat." He smiled.

"Doctor Jarreau is the best Preventionist I've ever gone to. He always gives me some fruit after my check-up."

I handed Haalima back her book. "I must go, my friends, so can we meet up this afternoon at the festival? I'm going to help set up."

"Yeah sure, of course." They snickered as they both took off running towards the sound of the freshly made ice cream cart. I heard the music cascading through the trees as I walked into the mail center.

"Why hello Nova, How's your family?"

"They are well, Mrs. Findlay."

"Well, what can I help you with today?"

"Can you see if my package has arrived? I want to pick it up before it goes out for drone delivery."

Mrs. Findlay's fingers began clicking on her holographic keyboard immediately, and just like that, she looked up from under her glasses.

"I'll be right back honey."

I was so excited I saved my credits all month for this dress and with the festival tonight maybe I'd run into Semyon. I blushed as I thought of our last encounter. I was at the beach and his friends had dared him to come over and talk to me, but I was so nervous I spilled my drink and ran off to the bathroom. How funny, but seeing it was the most important event in town for sure he would be there.

Mrs. Findlay reappeared with my box and quickly unwrapped it and placed the box into the reuse containers.

Covered in a silk bag I removed the dress, and it was as gorgeous as it seemed when I ordered it. I couldn't have been more pleased.

The silk was pristine. I had pondered over cotton or hemp but for this occasion, I had definitely chosen right. The purple, blue, and green fabric shimmered from its natural tints. Coming from the southern provinces of Pabulum Nation it was truly the best silk production and I was ready for an amazing festival night. I placed it in my reusable bag and said goodbye to Mrs. Findlay. Then skipped all the way home

thinking of how nice I'd look and if
Semyon would be there.

2

"Atten-Hut, cadets. it's time to get marching."

Semyon stretched and jumped to attention. The room was bustling with the hustle of young men throwing on their uniforms and scampering to the attention of Sergeant Miller's commands.

"FALL IN!"

"Today we are training for hydroelectric operations. After your mile run, we will meet at 1600 to discuss the building dynamics of our nation's various hydroelectric, solar, and turbine power systems." Sergeant Miller shouted.

"How they are built and how we can help maintain them."

"You will be trained to keep this nation's power-optimized and in harmony, so help me, Divine Architect."

"I will have you ready by the time you graduate, come hell or high water." Sergeant Miller snapped to attention and gave the cadets standing in formation their afternoon salute.

They then marched in unison out to the field to start their run.

"Psssst, Hey Semyon, hey wait up."

A young tall stocky cadet pushed his way through the lines of men trying to catch up, while still buttoning his uniform shirt.

"Hey, are you going to the festival after class?"

Pushing his coke bottle military glasses back onto his nose and practically tripping over his boots, he made his way to Semyon.

"I don't know Malo, hadn't really thought about it much. I've got Hydroelectric and engineering finals next week and you know if I ace those tests I'm up for promotion."

"Come on Semyon, you are always so structured, don't you want to go see what's going on in town and meet some girls?"

"I've been so ready to get Sergeant Miller's voice out of my head and have some fun."

"Graduation is in two months, Malo."

"I've got to stay focused. I'm trying to land a job at the Nation's Engineering Institute and if I pass all my finals with A's, it's a full ride."

"I can't do anything to mess this up." Semyon insisted.

"Come on Semyon, Geezzzz, you're practically the smartest person here." Malo huffed and puffed trying to keep up.

"Please, I've got to have someone to go with me to take leave. Please."

"You will ace your exams you know you will."

Just then Malo's boot hit the trail wrong, and he slammed face-first into the path.

"Semyon Please." He yelled as he sat up pushing his glasses back up on his nose.

 Malo was dusting the dirt off his uniform as a herd of young cadets jogged past him.

 "Sssssemyonnnnnn…."

Laughing Semyon picked up his stride.

He was top of his class at the Nation's guard, and with finals two months away he would be next in line for the esteemed internship position of Grand Engineer. A position that was among the most honored of any cadet graduating from the Nation's Guard.

In Pabulum Nation, young people had many choices of how they wanted to pursue their career paths. One could stay local, inherit, or be trained through apprenticeships for vocational and community careers; or one could go on to college which meant joining the Nation's Guard to be trained as Scientists, Technologists, Engineers, or

Mathematicians. The opportunities that synchronized which direction a person's life career choices were to be in Balance. The harmony of the Great Architect kept the Nation's people in power, water, housing, and food as these were the things crucial for ecological optimization.

Complete balance striving for both mankind and the planet as a discipline taught to each child from a very young age. Want not, waste not, a principle reminding us that every materialistic choice can lead to the reduction of waste. This lesson reverberated to keep our wants to a basic theory of "do you need that" and what will come to happen to these things when we no longer want them.

Our Nation had become optimized by making the things people wanted capable of either being recycled or composted. Unlike the dark years when humankind consumed and consumed with no consciousness of what would happen to their waste. The massive mountains of trash, described by Mr. Norman. Why did they not see their destruction? The ability to consume without any concern of the impact it would have on our planet.   The Great Architect taught our people it's ok to have things that you like or cherish. A pretty, new dress, or a nice new car, yet it was the responsibility of each person to know what impact their consumption has on our planet, our Mother Earth.

How those items are purchased and disposed of after their use has passed, was what Harmony and Balance meant. The basic knowledge, that we reap what we sow, and it is our duty as a species to care for the planet that cares for us.

Sacred Geometry teaches us that all things are connected and as the patterns of life are duplicated throughout the multiverse. We too are a basic component of those patterns. Honoring the ability to be creators to what lessons the earth illustrated. This was common knowledge to be in tune with our communities and our planet preserving the ecosystems, our honor. There was no other way.

Semyon knew that. He had graduated as a senior high valedictorian and his parents were so proud. He had finished writing his dissertation last semester on the hemp forests and their contribution to making materials that sustained the need for composites, used in technology, transportation, and industrialism. This concept allowed the nation the ability to make the country's products. These products made from hemp and bamboo materials were grown thus replenishing the earth's carbon back in the soil while giving the products the ability to be biodegradable and recyclable. A complete cycle of balance leaving the planet green and untainted by materialism.

Knowledge and philosophy were the driving force of all education centers in the nation as each child was taught to his or her own learning abilities. This ensured every person had their own unique kinship to their community's harmonious life journey. Semyon's education had led him to one of the nation's most pristine careers and in two months he would well be on his way to national leadership.

As Semyon whips around the final lap of his run, his blondish red hair was soaked with perspiration.

He thinks back to the girl he met at the beach, Nova.

It would be nice to see her.

Deciding then to stop and wait for Malo.

"Okay, Malo I'll go but just for a bit, then it's back to hitting the books."

"No more than an hour you hear me."

Huffing and puffing, Malo runs up pulling off his shirt and wipes the sweat off his chest.

Just then he hugs Semyon until his feet are off the ground.

"Uughhh." Uttered Semyon.

"I knew you had it in you. Thanks, my friend you won't regret it."

Malo dropped Semyon back on his feet.

"Now let's hit the showers and finish the day. I'll meet you at the dorm, say, 5 o'clock sharp."

Then he skips off like a little kid smiling and skipping all the way back to the showers.

Semyon couldn't help but shake his head and laugh. Malo was quite a character, but he was a good friend and tonight was going to be fun, he thought.

One night out on the town for the festival and some fun, a girl, then back to the books to launch his career.

What could happen?

3

The providence's streets are booming with people. Numerous tables are being beautifully decorated on Main Street with gorgeous hand-woven tablecloths. Flowers from all the local gardens are being arranged in dazzling glass vases for the finishing touches as the town's people hurry along to make the best effort for an amazing festival night. The solar lanterns are being hung from the trees by the Harmony

Volunteers, a local club that helps families who are having social issues or need community support, and the musicians are setting up the stage. Chefs from all over Pabulum Nation begin gathering in the community's outdoor kitchens to prepare for the feast of a lifetime, as local farmers carry in fresh food. Their contribution to the festivities. The town's center stage engulfed by the forest is normally a meeting place for the fine arts, music, poetry, and philosophy of the Divine Architect. However, now transformed into the most beautiful banquet of live decorations, flowers, candles, herbs, and tapestries. Each tapestry represents the different provinces of the nation. Among those steadily working, local breweries and winemakers set up their tap stations and the day is glistening with excitement, longing for the night. Compost bathrooms are set up for the influx of people and boxes of dishes made from hemp, that seed the earth after their end of use, are brought in. Finally, the dissipation crews bring in the recycling areas and everyone is getting close to being ready for the event.

A buzz of elation for what's to come is floating in the air as everyone works together to the hum of Mr. Norman's beat. Whistling along as he fiddled with the last tapestry to be hung.

"After the festival is over tomorrow, I'm going back to the dig." Mr. Norman hollered at Amida.

"You want to come? I am pretty sure I've come across an ancient library." Grinned Mr. Norman.

"But Mr. Norman, Isn't it dangerous down there." asked Amida.

"Danger is my middle name." Laughed Mr. Norman.

"I mean it could get dangerous but so far everything has been secure so, I'm going back tomorrow to bring out the books. Decades of hidden knowledge in those books, we might finally find out how the Great Shift started and when." He went back to whistling.

"Nova did you hear what Mr. Norman said?" Putting the finishing touches on one of my flower bouquets, Amida walks up.

"Did you hear what he said, Nova? A library. He said he was going tomorrow to start bringing up the books. Could you imagine if he finds out about what really happened?"

"I want to go Nova. I want to go tonight. I can't wait to see what the books say."

"It's almost 5 o'clock, Amida have you lost your mind? The festival is starting in an hour and Haalima will be here soon. I've got to run back to the house and change into my new dress."

I said goodbye for now to everyone and went back to the house to get ready. Just then there is a knock at the door.

"Hello, Haalima, I heard Elisa say. Come on in."

"Nova is in her room, go on back."

"Nova, can I come in?" Sure Haalima.

"Are you excited about tonight?" She asked.

"I am so excited. Do you think Semyon will be there?"

"I don't know, I haven't seen him since summer break when we were all at the beach. You know he's stationed in Southern Provence. It's only an hour's drive from here so maybe he'll come for the Harmony awards. After all, it's not like this happens every day."

"Do you like my dress, Nova? My Mom made it for me."

"It's beautiful Haalima."

 "You look so beautiful, let me help you with your hair."

Her dress was a pastel pink with finely embroidered flowers that must have taken her mother hours to sew. The cotton flowing softly off her shoulders just as the chocolate curls of her hair cascade around her neck.

"A few bobby pins and there you look gorgeous." I declared.

"I see you are still curious about Semyon." She giggled.

"After last summer I thought for sure you'd forgotten all about him."

"Haalima, I am just curious that's all." Rolling my eyes and hiding my blushing grin.

"What's up with you and Amida anyway?" I distractedly changed the subject.

"I thought you two were quite the item."

"Yeah, I did too but he's going to the Nation's Guard next month, so we've decided to break it off."

"This is a big decision for him, and you know I'll be staying here to work the gardens. So, we don't know what else to do. He'll be gone for two years when he enlists but after that, he'll be well on his way to the life of a computing scientist and well I'll be here, farming."

"Not sure how that will work but we do care for each other, so we've just decided to see other people."

"Ughhh, it's so hard to date these days she laughed. I don't know, maybe there will be some cute boys there tonight and I'll get my mind off this whole Amida thing."

"Dancing and singing that's all I want to think about tonight, Nova."

She was finishing the last touches of her makeup made from honey and rose petals that smelled so nice, when I looked up at the clock.

 "Haalima, we must go, or we are going to be late."

 "As usual." she laughed.

"Let's go." I grabbed a crocheted shawl and checked myself out in the mirror one more time.

Holding hands, we were rushing out the door.

"Have a great evening, girls." Elisi said softly, so as not to wake Robyn, who had fallen asleep. Her little head nestled on Elisi's lap.

"Don't stay out too late." She smiled. "Love you."

"Love you too Elisa, and we won't."

As we ran up the street, we could hear the festival. The musicians tuning their instruments. The Sounds of people talking and the smell of food cooking in the kitchens. All the senses were alive with festivity as the crowds began to assemble.

Just then a sharp shriek of a microphone pierced my eardrums as the mayor walked onto the stage. Behind him is a group of well-dressed folks. They must have been the committee from the Gardens of Greta.

"Hello everyone and wel…..."

The microphone went in and out and was then accompanied by loud muffled taps.

"Hello everyone and welcome to this year's Harmony Awards. I would like to thank the judges for coming all the way to Plethora to announce the winner of the prestigious Harmony Awards. We would like to say thank you to the representatives from the 13 provinces for their contributions."

He then turned and bowed to the various providence leaders as they in turn bowed back.

"As you all know this year we also are among the nominees and with all statistics in and accounted for we will soon know who the winners are. Please feel free to eat, drink and be merry. In approximately one hour we will announce the optimization results, so maestro let's play some music."

He gestured to the band and the area was teeming with the sounds of drums, to preclude the horns, and then the strings. A young girl, no more than fifteen, began to sing. Her voice echoing through the streets with the most beautiful song of our city and the quest our people took to honor the Divine Architect.

The food was carried out in droves of fish, shrimp, crabs, scallops, and oysters. The fresh seafood came first. Next beautifully decorated plates of duck, quill, turkey, and rabbit. Then the meat venison and boar with vegetable melodies from the gardens in every assortment a chef could create. The beef was sliced and presented as our most special occasion feast saved for only the times when the community was altogether. This was to stay in harmony with the herd management and land preservation. The smells of fine foods linger in the wind as the dishes are arranged on the tables. Herbs such as mint, basil, thyme, garlic, and lemongrass envelop the senses and rumbling the tummy. As lines for handwashing and dinner began to form the elders proceeded to the dance floor. It was tradition for the town leaders to have the first dance before returning to take care of the festival's preparatory measures.

"I wish Elisi could still dance at the festival Haalima. I miss seeing her dance since she has gotten up in age." I giggled.

"Nova, your Elisi is 98 years old. You know she would be here if she could." Haalima knocked her elbow into mine and we laughed.

We both squeezed our way to the dance floor to watch a spectacular performance of skill and grace as our elders swooshed each other around the central courtyard.

Just then vaguely across the floor, was that real? I caught a glimpse of blondish red hair wildly uncombed or at least styled to look that way. I tried to focus through the spinning gowns of our elder's choreography.

"Haalima look, I think I see Semyon." I looked her in the face, eyes wide whispering.

"Is that him?"

"Yes, I think it is." She grabbed my hands and laughed.

"Who is he with? I've never seen that guy before?"

"I don't know Haalima."

"Let's go get in line for dinner so maybe we can run into them." I suggested.

Laughing and giggling like we were in third grade again.

"Nova, the lady's room is right behind them, let's just head that way." She winked and grabbed the ribbons on my dress.

"Let's go, follow my lead." She said as we wedged our way through the groups of people standing around the dance floor. Lost in the crowd, it seemed like forever jostling our way through the masses.

"Can you see them, Haalima?"

She was a good three inches taller than me, and I was nervous.

Our last encounter was quite embarrassing, so I had to play it cool this time.

Suddenly her hand slipped from mine, and she was gone, enveloped by the crowd. I excused myself properly and could see her head bobbing up and down a few people ahead of me, heading out of the central courtyard towards the bathrooms.

"Nova, Nova is that you?"

I felt a soft tap on my shoulder.

I stopped cold, knowing who the voice belonged to.

"It's me, Semyon, from the beach. You remember, don't you?"

I slowly turned around on my tiptoes much like a ballerina spinning oh so slowly in a pirouette.

My head spinning in the thought of, oh my Divine Architect, where is Haalima?

Nervous and blushing.

"Oh Hey, Semyon, yes, of course, I remember you." I smiled.

"Hey, well um, how are you, how have you been?" My voice, shy and unsure.

"I'm good, this is Malo. He is my friend from the Guard."

Without warning, I feel two hands on my shoulders, and I hear Haalima jumping up and down behind me.

"Hey, I'm Haalima."

"Hey, yeah, so how's it going, yeah, um, I said that already." I timidly smiled.

"Geez, Nova." Haalima pushed me to the side to formally introduce herself to Malo.

"Hi, was it, Malo?"

"I'm Haalima." She shook his hand with a big cheesy smile.

"Look, the elders are leaving the dance floor."

"Up for a twirl around the floor Malo?"

"Why yes, my lady." And they were off with a spin to frolic.

"Well, hey, Semyon, how are your studies going?"

I stood there not really sure where to even start the conversation.

"They are going great, Nova. I'm up for the internship position of Grand

Engineer in two months, as long as, I ace my finals, of course."

He kept his hands in his golden locks as he spoke.

"That's great Semyon your family must be……"

Abruptly, Mr. Norman interrupted the conversation.

"I'm sorry kids, have you seen Amida."

"….so Proud." I concluded.

"He was supposed to help me backstage for the concert." He sighed with perplexity.

"I've been looking everywhere.

I even tried his locator."

"Nothing." He grabbed a handkerchief out of his pocket, wiped his forehead and took back off towards the stage yelling over the crowd.

"If you see him, will you please tell him to get his rear end backstage?"

Nova paused to think of the last time she saw Amida.

"Oh no Semyon, the last thing Amida said to me was that he didn't want to wait till tomorrow to go to the dig."

"Dig? Nova?"

"Oh yeah, Mr. Norman and some of the Archeological Society are unearthing a dig. Mr. Norman thinks it's an ancient Library from the Dark Ages."

"We had a field trip there and Haalima brought out a few books."

"Amida has been consumed with curiosity ever since."

"Do you really think he would go down there alone this close to the celebration?" Semyon asked, puzzled. Still running his hands through his hair.

"How far away is it?"

"Like 10 minutes from here on the west side of town." I answered.

Semyon gestured across the dance floor to get Malo's attention. Waving his arm high in the air until Malo and Haalima noticed and started heading towards us.

They both were laughing and still breathing heavily from the fast pace of the crowded dance floor.

"Haalima, Mr. Norman said Amida didn't show up to help him backstage."

She was still laughing and looking at Malo smiling. I could see she was annoyed I would bring up Amida while she was having so much fun.

"Haalima, the last thing he said to me was that he couldn't wait till tomorrow to go back to the dig."

Malo was still spinning Haalima to the music when she completely stopped and rolled her eyes at me.

"Nova, do you mean to tell me you think he went to the dig?"

"Tonight?"

"Of all nights?"

"He was very adamant. I thought he would wait." I explained, having felt a bad feeling in the pit of my stomach.

"The way he was acting was peculiar. I thought it was just you know…. Haalima."

Not wanting to divulge too much information.

"What dig and who is Amida?" Malo interjected.

Semyon spoke up. "He is a friend we all knew from the beach and there's an archeological dig."

"Cool." Snickered Malo.

"Not cool." Grumbled Haalima under her breath.

"He's kind of my ex-boyfriend."

"Oh." Muttered Malo. With a confused look.

"Well, if we hurry, we can all just go for a walk and see if we see him. We will still be back in time for the reveal and celebration." Expressed Semyon.

"It shouldn't take us long and it will put all your minds to ease."

"No worries. Let's go."

He was so confident, how could I say no.

4

As we walked through the orchards of the wood line path, we came to a clearing. The dig site didn't look like much from the trail. Some sticks and strings and piles of dirt. Of course, there was now a cave-like entrance. The same cavern Mr. Norman kept popping in and out of when we came here on the field trip. A row of tables under a tent held screens and water buckets for washing, studying, and cataloging items retrieved. Hemp cloth was laid over the site to keep it safe from the weather and the forest.

There were storage containers that held the artifacts that had been brought up. Even a special storage container, because some of the things they were bringing up were contaminated and had to be specially disposed of.

Luckily, the area had been strung with solar lights so there was enough light to navigate the area without getting dirty. I hoped we would find Amida quickly and get back in time for the ceremony.

The cave-like entrance was lit up. We could see down a bit, until the light faded around a slight curve. Solar light systems ran off each other so the lights outside sent energy to the ones placed inside the cave.

Semyon and Malo were excited like young boys playing king of the mountain. Hopping around the dirt piles at the entrance of the cave.

"We shouldn't go in there." I cautioned, standing next to Haalima directly at the entrance.

The boys jump down from the piles of dirt to inspect the entrance mound.

"Look there! Can you see it, it's a satchel of some sort?" Malo took off into the cave.

Grabbing Haalima's hand without even moving. I glanced over at Semyon, both of us knowing we were about to step foot into the unknown.

His charismatic grin and bright eyes are ever so adventurous, and I wonder what is to come next.

The three of us chase Malo down the hall.

He has a satchel in his hand and most definitely it is Amida's.

Around the curve, we can see a ladder disappearing into a hole in the ground and Amida's jacket tossed next to it.

"I can't believe he did this." Haalima shrieks.

"How could he go down there tonight?"

"We are missing the reveal." She unwittingly knew one of us had to see if he was okay. We now knew he was down there.

"This is so selfish of him, Geez." She agonized. "You know someone must go see if he's alright."

"We'll all go." I concluded. It wasn't fair to send just the boys.

We would all have to go. It was the only way to stay safe. Staying together.

Semyon and Malo were now inspecting the void with flashlights they found lying on a nearby supply table.

"I'll go first, I don't mind." Announced Malo. Holding on to the ladder looking back at us.

"We are trained for this." He reassured us with a smile. Pushing his glasses back up on his nose.

Semyon looked at me with a sign of assurance that everything was going to be ok.

"We have 25 minutes before the reveal." Semyon asserted.

"It's going to be okay, Nova."

"Besides, what is down there?"

"I'm curious as well." Thrilled Malo, and down the ladder he went.

Next was Haalima, Semyon helping her so gently.

"Are you ready Nova?" He reached for my hand, then ever so tenderly placing his hands on my hips, helped me step over the edges of the ravine to reach ahold of the ladder.

One foot after another, down I went into the excavation.

It took a few seconds for my eyes to adjust. It is dark and musty. The dust is thick to breathe. I am not sure how many steps I took but it seemed to go down forever.

Ever so careful, I pace my steps holding tight to the rungs.

Suddenly, I began to see what appeared to be shelves; rows of tall bookcases seeming to hold up the roof, we had apparently entered the room from. They are crumbled in some areas, holding what came into view as piles of dust, where rows of books once laid.

Placed throughout the ground area were a set of lights much like the ones in the hall but dimmer.

I could finally see the bottom, so things began to come into focus as I stepped firmly onto the floor.

As I step back and look up, Semyon is right behind me only steps away from reaching the floor.

Haalima and Malo are already snooping around the tables set up by the Archeological Society piled with artifacts, we have never seen before.

I inspect my dress for any traces of dirt. As adventurous and exciting as my time with Semyon was, I wanted to dance and trying to stay clean was going to be impossible down here.

I wanted to get back to the ceremonies as soon as possible, without anyone knowing I had ever been gone.

"Amida!" Haalima yelled.

The sound of her voice echoing loudly throughout the immense hollow space.

"AMIDA!"

Semyon and Malo had ventured to one of the tall bookcases and were inspecting the shelves.

Semyon bends down and puts his head close to the spine of the book, squinting to make out the words.

Legal Catalog Vol 59. It read.

The books were semi-in-line still with multiple columns intact until the shelf ended in which they lay in a crumpled mess on the floor.

"What are these?" Questioned Malo.

"They are Law books." Semyon Replied.

"I guess the people of this time had an incredible number of books about Laws. Look at all these columns."

He reached out to pick one up just as a loud roaring voice came out of the shadows.

"NOOOOOO! Don't touch those ones."

It was Amida, trying to stop Semyon. But it was too late, and just as he looks down at the books again a chain reaction of disintegration, much like a push of the dominos, the books are now a pile of dust.

"Ohhh No." Cried Amida.

"What have you done?"

"What have I done!" Rebuked Semyon.

Haalima interjected at that point.

"Amida what are you, oh my Divine Architect, what are you doing?" She shouted Lividly.

"Haalima, you are not going to believe what I found." He bolstered.

"Amida that is not what she meant." I reworded the question.

"Why are you down here Amida?"

"Why are you down here now?"

"The reveal is starting, like, right now."

"Oh yeah, so I can see her all night, dancing and having fun without me. No way, I've been wanting to get down here anyway."

Haalima blushes and looks at Malo and shrugs.

"Nova, all this aside you must see this."

"We can come back tomorrow, Amida, with Mr. Norman, who by the way, is pretty upset you didn't show up to help him backstage at the concert."

"Ok but Nova, everyone, I found some sort of headquarters. Not like the library itself but something different. I don't think anyone has seen it. I want to show you."

"You can show us tomorrow Amida let's go." I demanded.

Then with a sigh of relief, I ushered Amida and everyone back towards the ladder. We were going to make it back in time. I was relieved.

Malo, of course, went first. Then Haalima.

I could see they were almost halfway up when Amida let out a loud screech.

"Wait, I forgot something." He ran back towards the shadows.

"A journal." He hollered as he dipped out of sight.

Semyon and I look up and we can still see Malo and Haalima when a tremendous creek compels our attention.

Everyone's attention.

Malo, and Haalima freeze looking up and down at each other.

I look into Semyon's eyes normally blue and kind, now anticipative much like a deer frozen in headlights.

The horrid creak again bellowed as we began to see the bookcase that held the books turned to dust, waiver.

I motioned to Semyon without words. We ran. Looking up to see what may happen to our vulnerable friends clinging to the ladder in the air. Holding on as tight as they could.

Gasping for air, I uncovered my head. I didn't see the exact method the roof fell. But as the dust settled, I crawled out from under a table where I had sought shelter from what seemed to be equivalent to a blast.

The bookcase that fell was holding up the roof and when it came down half the ceiling and earth came down with it.

I coughed and wiped my eyes, calling softly to my friends.

"Semyon, Haalima, Malo, Amida? Where is everyone?"

I could hear a cough and rustle from under some debris.

With all my might, I lift the broken pieces of the ceiling, recovering Malo.

He was covered with dust and debris. His glasses were still on his face but cracked.

As I looked him over, I could see a trail of blood.

Starting to panic, I feel the comfort of Semyon's hands on my shoulder.

"Is he ok?" He asked.

"He's bleeding. Where is Haalima?"

"I'm over here." I hear a faint voice say.

"Are you ok?" I asked.

"A few cuts and bruises but I'm very fortunate to be alive." She is now walking closer.

"My leg is broken." Said Malo coughing.

We can see the relief in each other's faces that he is conscious.

My dress is ruined, so I tear just enough fabric off the hem to make a bandage. While Haalima and Semyon attempt to move him.

"Ughhhhh." Malo cries out in pain as we leverage and hoist him to a clear area.

"Where is Amida, Nova?" Haalima's eyes are full of tears.

"I don't know. Let's get Malo stable and we will look for him together."

"I'm going to see if I can find a way out, okay girls?" Semyon announced.

"Wait, we need to stick together." I urged.

"Please, we must find Amida after we help Malo."

"Okay, Nova, what can I do?" He stopped and wiped the dirt off my cheek.

"Please, first let's try to stop the bleeding."

"Are you still with us Malo?"

"Yes, mam." He whispered.

The shockwave knocks Amida off his feet as he runs back into the ancient makeshift headquarters. Tremors shake the room allowing particles of dust and dirt to fall from the ceiling, vibrating books and papers onto the floor. Amida turns back to check on his friends, but a mountain of debris blocks the exit to the main room, and he is trapped. A large desk sits in the middle of the room covered in what looked like ancient computing systems. The screens were black and covered in dust and cobwebs; these devices were just so crude and bulky. He thought.

In Pabulum Nation computing is quantum, thus networked and holographic. Installed in every home, business, and public area. One only had to speak to access information, communications, location, or memory. Transportation includes self-driving and graphical interface systems thus optimizing carbon and planetary climate control.

Unfortunately, they were trapped far off the grid, and with everyone at the festival, well, who would even know to look for them. Amida thought. This was all his responsibility and if he had just waited for Mr. Norman. He shook his head sitting on the ground with his head still between his knees.

And what of his friends?

He looked around the room. This room was different from the others. While the main parts of the library seemed to be formal. This room conveyed the impression of a headquarters or command center. The desk in the center, the computing systems. The brain of the operations.

Two walls were covered with bookshelves while the other two were covered with images and papers held on my small colorful tacks. Each tack drawing lines of string to each other in a connected plot. All leading to a map of the earth in the center. There are pictures of people and articles with headlines.

Amida searched around for the journal he had found earlier. It was dusty and ripped on the hardback cover. Inside lines of blue with writing on them. Small sketches were placed within the pages, and it seemed to be chronicles of a woman's life work. The pages were handwritten and hard to make out.

Handwriting, now often practiced as an art form, was the language of the past. Replaced by computations and networks of the Architect Divine. An interconnected optimization of connectivity that kept our Nation in Balance and Harmony with our ecosystem to preserve our Mother Earth. It was a perfect system of data that monitored the masses while aiding the individuals it maintained.

Amida, points his flashlight at the dusty pages and begins to make out the words.

Mira was written all over the front cover in different swirly patterns. Mira loves Tristian. In every heart like drawing, one could imagine.

He gently pulled open the cover and began to read.

Mira's Journal

I was born in 1983 in Camp
Pendleton, California.

My father was a United States Marine and,

I was his champion.

Somehow, sometime in the past our family became part of the Originals.

They were the first families to devise a formula for money transfer that they believed would save future generations from tyranny.

Training their children as a secret society of soldiers they believed would protect the world.

They were wrong, the series of events they created would be the fall of America.

The divisions of families that in turn, lead to the rise of darkness.

This is my story.

Memories

Everyone has memories when you think back and remember the good and the bad.

Much like a movie that plays in your mind.

Saving thoughts and emotions to be locked away until you retrieve them.

These memories shape the person we become.

Are those memories good or bad?

And

When you raise a child in pain, poverty and suffering will they turn out wholesome?

Good or vice versa?

This simple question has been cited so many times throughout history.

Nature versus Nurture?

Discussed, philosophized, studied, and emulated to create a basic formula.

A formula that would create social order.

Encompassed in our memories.

As I see it, this was the basis of the Originals thought process.

Simply raise a child in the beginning years with no limitations allowing them to be who they choose on a subconscious level.

During that time implanting the mind with memories.

I would be allowed to make choices that shaped me, naturally evolving on my own.

Each decision was shaped by whether I would choose right or wrong.

What is wrong?

Are you bad if you make bad choices and can this be measured?

Does a child sin?

During this time my memories, grandma cooking in the kitchen, the first crush I experienced, the first time I fell off my bike, these memories saved in my mind forever.

Not only my mind, but the Original's mind as well.

The study of hindsight science reared its evil head.

Hindsight is 20:20, the saying goes, able to see in clarity the path one chooses only in the reflection of our thoughts.

The Originals studied this process as ways to find what they believed is truly in a person's heart.

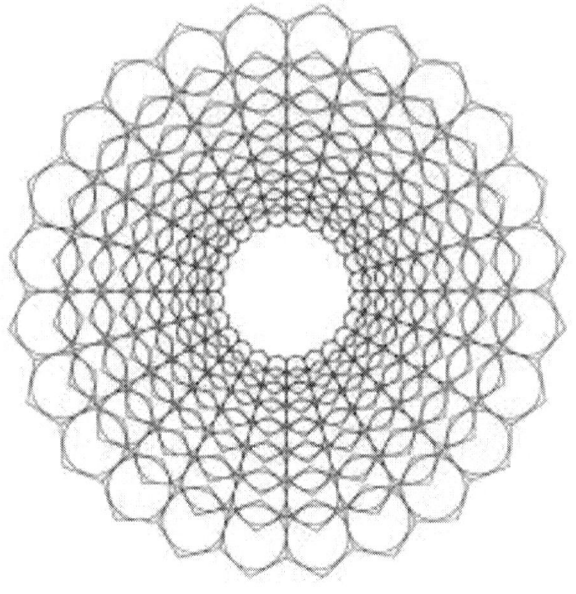

Choices

Consider for a moment that while presented with choices, memories can have a significant influence on a person.

What about mistakes?

Does a person make a choice based on the subconscious?

Are those choices based on secret wants and desires or are they shaped by triggers from the past?

This is how the formula worked.

Recording and studying the choices a person makes, as a means, to their soul.

Accessing those emotions by means of our memories.

All those memories saved collaborated and focused into a system of judgment by a society of shepherds.

The shepherds, also challenged by the process.

The same survival of their memories,

good and bad that shaped their thoughts and emotions.

A system of entanglement, all intertwined in a formula of traditions, a game of sorts where there were no winners.

Only the carnage of the families left to share the pain of their dead loved ones like a badge of honor.

The strength of their family to overcome.

At least the ones that made it.

Where was there any room for God?

Religion had caused so many wars and the removal of that mindset was the goal of the shepherds.

The shepherds were your everyday people who had survived their own awakening.

Each person awakened in a format unique to their own experiences.

Their own personal accumulation of thoughts.

Basically, if you survived the trials and tribulations of the awakening process you were deemed to be a shepherd, a guardian.

There were levels in which a person could rise the ranks, but it all started with the Baptism of Fire.

Most people entered this process young, unless their families were legacies, like mine.

"Every family has a crazy one", my father once said.

The crazy one was the person they deem to be a champion. Feeding you to the wolves as prey for the hunt, regardless I would come back leading the pack.

In this secret society, the formula was to distribute wealth without inheritance.

The result, the making of soldiers of one's own children, fighting for the chance to win life with inheritance.

When a person entered an awakening, it was the goal of the entire community to grade and deem the person essential to society or outcast.

A color, animal, and element usually were assigned during this process.

Most importantly though was the assignment of social-economic wealth, marriage arrangements, and life expectancy.

If you were an outcast, you are deemed unworthy of opportunity and advancement, unless you were pretty, which meant you would be upgraded or sold to the rich.

In my case, I was sold to the dark side to ensure my sister's marriage advancement.

Outcasts could also be used to create outlaw personalities which would reinforce a society of conformity.

That society now needs governing systems of control for economic profit, hence jails, penitentiaries, and asylum, which are booming businesses.

I look back and imagine how it all must have started.

A simple wager that sparked an idea.

That idea snowballs into something out of control.

Coming to a new country where land, resources, and potential possibilities were abundant, our ancestors must have seen how this privilege had affected their children.

Money can tear families apart, and oh, so well, did privilege often reflects badly on children who were raised with everything their hearts desired.

Two men sitting at a fire enjoying a cigar.

," I bet if your son and my daughter can stay married for a set amount of time while being cut off from the family, then and only then would they be worthy to inherit such wealth."   Mr. Smith said.

"I see your point," said Mr. Jones

"How about I take that wager but with one condition? ".

"I get to tell my daughter what to say and do for that time period."

Mr. Smith thought about it for a few minutes.

"Ok, but I get to do the same for my son."

"Sounds like a deal," Mr. Jones said.

"Now let's agree to the terms.

Let's agree to, say, eleven years".

"The length of the Iliad."

"If your child leaves or dies, I will pay the inheritance to you.

If my child leaves or dies, you will pay the inheritance to me and if they make it happily.

Well then, they will receive the full inheritance and be free to live out their lives as a very wealthy husband and wife."

Just like that, the world had changed.

Something so simple.

You can imagine the elaborate lengths each family went through to deceive or manipulate the poor young couple?

Elaborate scenarios began to involve the entire community as many towns in those days were small and mostly family.

Would the couple make it, what challenges would they face?

The seven sins are picked as basic moral guidelines.

If each child could face the temptations of the bible and prosper, then they would indeed be worthy of such wealth.

It was most definitely a great idea for a simpler wholesome world.

Families love the game.

The possibility of watching a young couple overcome and bloom into honorable members in their community, worthy of such gifts, entices the lot of them.

Keeping also in mind the friendly competition that motivated everyone to work a little harder, succeed a little more.

Times were tough, strength was a virtue, and for a young couple surviving in early America while enduring the family traditions,

This life was normal.

What could possibly go wrong?

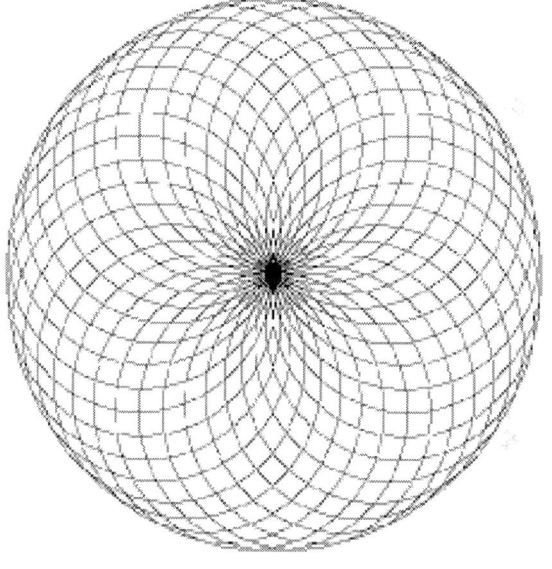

War

Slavery is what goes wrong., A formula of social control created by Willie Lynch is devised for slaves and freed slaves to impose total government control.

A formula that is bolstered will repeat for a thousand years once implemented.

The Civil War breaks out and families become divided.

The nation is in turmoil.

Blood covers America: homes, plantations, businesses, and resources are in rubble.

The forefathers are desperate
for the fighting to end.

But no one can agree.

War without bloodshed, war
without loss of economic
structures.

A Civil War, civil as in we can still
be at war, but we can do it a
different way.

The formula created by Lynch for
social control is now not only
subjected to slaves but now to the
entire population.

By now, many families practice the Marriage Morality game.

The benefits are a custom rather than a tradition, but political families who are hurt, angry, and are deep seeded in Masonic roots begin to think of ways to calm a nation, yet exact revenge, wealth, and power.

The formula is adopted into tradition.

Thirteen families see themselves as superior.

Separating themselves from the rest.

The Original 13 colonies of The United States of America. Descended from royal blood, they began to devise a plan that involves the same guidelines of the marriage morality game, now mixed with the formula of social control.

This is the birth of American espionage and spies are born.

Breeding and inheritance could now include traditions and strategies to create order.

This order rendered into a new tradition that solidified bloodlines keeping the money, power, and influence contained into the competition of the Trinity.

The trinity, the father-son, and the wholly ghost.

The families were divided into four teams.

This kept the wealth balanced between them by means of marrying children from feuding families into holy matrimony.

Competing for the wealth of the next generation. one family stayed out to be treasurer, rotating each tide.

Family members became treasures representing each family.

This process would ensure the formula designated the family's inheritance without hostility and destruction.

Training the future's children, unaware they were operatives, now referred to as salt.

The thought process was as such, what happens when two people marry from families that hate each other?

Would love prevail?

What of life with an adversarial plot to alleviate tensions yet keep the bloodlines pure.

How could this process save the families in an unstable nation?

Only by keeping to the code could the families participate and so a strict moral guideline was adopted.

They would never, not ever speak of this, it was agreed.

Not in plain English but only by code.

One member of each family was chosen as their champion.

Although starting out with married couples, families who had no children to marry also began an interest in the game.

Firstborns were likely to be the first choice, but some families saw it as the favorite child, the best candidate.

Quoting the bible John 3:16, "for God so loved the world that he gave his one and only son, that whoever believes in him shall not perish but have eternal life."

If God could sacrifice his only son who could argue with that.

And what of everlasting life, who could resist?

In a country deep seeded in religious beliefs, it seemed plausible to test this theory.

The Power of Suggestion

The power of suggestion became
the term of the hunt.

Communities were small back then
and everyone made the sacrifice to
live in the realm of the hunt.

Civilized warfare to shape a
person into what was at the heart
of their subconscious.

Armed with memories a test now
of

Strength vs weakness.

How does one determine what's in
a person's heart?

The fundamental question of good vs. evil and saint vs. the outlaw.

The power of suggestion was devised to reach the depth of that issue.

Much like planting seeds in the mind of those who are undetermined to make their own choices.

Were those seeds to bloom into a beautiful garden of roses or were they to become weeds that must be plucked from society?

The champions presented to common townsfolk thus each encountered a testament of the true nature of that intention.

People would make subtle statements to see how the person would be shaped.

The influences carving and shaping the champion's personality based on predetermined prejudice or simple open-mindedness.

Each encounter presents a chance that could be assessed in a choice that could lead to both a positive and negative option.

Allowing each person the opportunity for advancement in a position of light or opportunity to follow a path of darkness.

The families divide their team's champions into the Dark and the Light.

For even darkness has its place in the world and could be used to subjugate the plans of the light.

The dark became our Outlaws and a new need for systems of societal judgment.

Structures of control are
implemented.

The birth of these systems gives
rise to those judgments for profit,
hence penitentiaries, jails, and
asylums.

If people chose the path of
darkness they must be governed
by the light.

The Awakening

I was 34 years old before I was awakened.

The oldest ever to be Baptized by Fire.

I'm sure it was the intention of my family that I was never to be awakened but after two failed marriages you begin to see the world differently.

I began to see coincidences in everyday life that didn't seem to add up.

Patterns in people's behaviors that were recurring throughout my life.

Apparently, my parents were hunters.

Part of the Original Legacies whose families carried out these traditions as far back as seven generations of first eldest daughters.

I often wondered why they didn't wake me and was later told it was because of the sexual abuse I suffered as a very young child.

Used as bait for the hunt, the predator, our neighborhood mailman.

He had been molesting children
for half his life and was not caught
until the age of seventy.

When the predator took the bait, I
had given my first sacrifice.

I was left to believe in a world free
and just.

Much like the songs we sing about
America.

I believed this was the land of the
free.

Home of the brave.

All that disillusion ended in the
failure of my second marriage.

To be sealed by the marriage of
my father to a younger woman.

My life would never be the same.

I couldn't believe the strength I
possessed to overcome the fire.

Although I was sent to my
demise, the chances were to win
the hunt. If one succeeded it was a
rebirth of sorts, to be included
back in the family or so I thought.

The generations skipped with
inheritance so most of my future
was used up by my ex-husbands,
children, and the rest to my
father's new bride.

It worked much like a passing
down of personalities if you have
ever heard someone say:

"you're just like your grandmother
or your just like your uncle",

That's how they start the process.

People hear that and assign you
roles based on the estate of the
person in mention.

My entire life people have said
"you're just like your mother".

I never understood because I was
raised by my father, who was

single, and no one really knew my
mother.

It seemed I was doomed to take
that role and that was a role I
refused to accept.

It was hard for me at my age to see
the world so differently.

Waking up to the fact that life was
different.

Not understanding that America
was not free; it was controlled by
families who assigned your life as a
value.

Deemed whether you were worthy of the price tag put on your head and decidedly sending you to the hunt if you were not.

I had been unknowingly sold at the age of 17 to the dark when I had my first daughter.

This union would set my sister up for life in a proper marriage with the light and send my life in a spiral of pain and heartache.

Used for the hunt.

That was until I met Him.

The Hunt

I have been hunted for so long it
seems like the world before never
even existed.

Normal people, your friends, work
relationships all over at the drop of
a hat.

The hunt is on.

So, that value they place on your
life, well, it becomes money the
family can use, if they no longer
want you.

The shady gambling deals in the
background.

The power of suggestions to persuade you to loosen your morals.

All those aspects form a price of what the shepherds and higher up regard your life to be worth.

This price is subjective to whoever's morals that you are enthralled by.

The traditions of the past, the rules they follow.

If your community is filled with shepherds that are loving and kind you could excel. But,

If your shepherds were hard and callous.

Obsessed with gambling and control, you may not excel.

I did very well for myself owning my own spa for the middle part of my life.

My community saw how hard I worked to achieve my goals and I was rewarded.

Blessed, they call it.

Some things are just out of your control, sickness, my husband's infidelity, the series of events that lead to the end of my second marriage.

My first marriage was over when I was barely 25.

Broken bones to my face.

My family decided I was unworthy of their kindness, ultimately sending me back to the hunt.

Completely blind to the knowledge it even existed.

Here I was, lost on an island, sad and alone.

My husband, children were taken.

I was recovering from illness, and unemployed for the first time since I was 13.

I wandered to the beach and just sat there contemplating.

I had never really been the type you could hold down for long.

I was a thinker and a doer, someone who always saw the possibilities where some people saw none.

I set out to rebuild myself on my own.

Little did I know, again I was just the bait.

The island, the arena, and the beach well, that was the watering hole.

The place where hunters and their families came to select their next meal.

Unknowingly, my preconditioning thought process began to tick and unhealthy cycles that hunter's prey on began to emerge.

Drinking, smoking, and partying,

I was on an island of misfit toys, I told myself, and while in Rome.... God, I just want a cigarette, sucks being hunted.

The mere mention of smoking and I am reminded that being hunted sucks.

The first thing they attack is your vices.

Smoking is the one true vice I struggle with.

The rest, I could give or take, but smoking was a bad habit,

I just couldn't kick.

Your vices were the first thing
that made you feel crazy, beers,
wine, cigarettes, certain foods.

No matter what your thing was, all
of a sudden it was different.

If it brought you comfort or you
were accustomed to it had
suddenly changed.

Once the things you were
accustomed to change, one would
think to ask around.

Does this seem different to you?

But seeing every person around you is hunting you, you can bet your ass that no one will agree.

Gaslighting is the term.

The code dictates don't ever speak of it., but

Keep your head up, you're not alone.

The breakdown of the moral compass.

The goal of the hunters through the power of suggestion; through the removal of the tolerances, you never knew you had.

All seemingly small shards to a larger whole, that whole being the person who you are at the core of your heart and soul.

Once I entered the hunt as prey, long-time friendships, and relationships, even your parents, your children become people to add confusion to your life.

Seeing you now as a value, that would be passed to them if you were consumed by the darkness,

Or a champion, the legacy of their family.

Through hindsight, everyday conversations began to encompass simple phrases that trigger memories.

Spinning a person's mind in confusion.

People familiar with your hopes and fears and insecurities begin to break down your morality.

Suggesting options to cloud your judgment.

Some families have turned this into an art creating an entire language designed to guide you in the wrong direction.

People who are easily gullible don't last long in the arena.

While others excel at the art of manipulation, leaving the broken-hearted in their wake.

Some families work in packs destroying any hope a simple or kind person could have, leaving them with the suggestion that taking their own lives would be a sacrifice for the greater good.

Memories, suggestions, and symbolism that are all designed to plant seeds,

Seeds of doubt, fear, suspicion, and paranoia.

Confusing and invasive, clouding what is real and what is not.

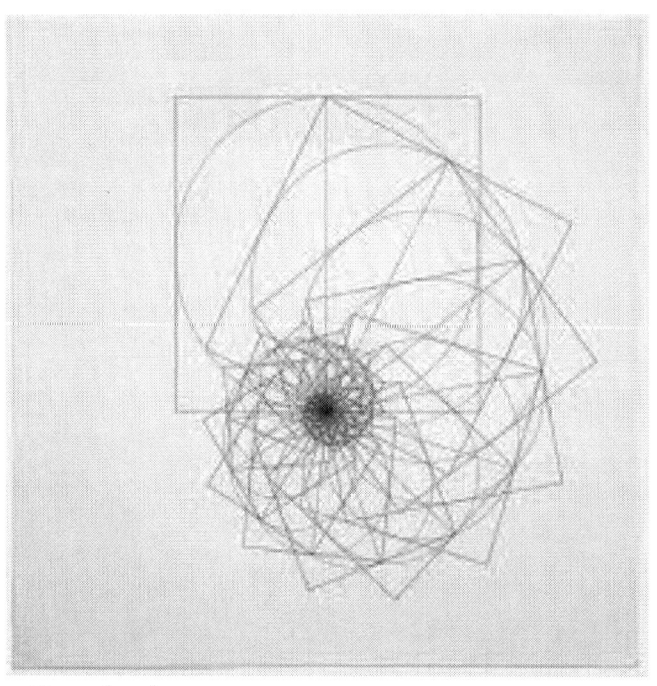

Symbolism

Symbolism is the root of the system.

Once devised by our ancestors, the system motivated stories and movies, formed outlaws, both good and bad characters creating legends.

Today in an age of marketing and the internet, Symbolism is the sign of the beast, the mechanism that drives the game and fuels the hunt.

Everyday symbols encoding images that represent different things to different people.

A simple bumper sticker that reminds one of a moment lost in time.

License plates that spread messages of love or hate.

Everywhere you look the world has systemized our market strategies into messages that literally talk to a person, seemingly transmitting thoughts and feelings.

The strong learn to live with the messages, standing firm in their convictions.

The weak, weeded out by the inability to stay focused through the constant barrage of mixed messages.

The internet has been the most lethal in a new world of technology.

Hunters become hackers and infiltrate a person's life in full disguise and comfort of a keyboard.

I call them keyboard warriors.

Once infiltrated into your system of operation suggestive programs games and marketing symbolism can be applied.

Targeting the prey much faster.

All the while, protecting these people from any emotional responses of their prey.

The bigger the emotional response a hunter can invoke the better the families are in a test of strength.

Who can appear as if everything is completely normal, and these so-called coincidences are not happening?

In hindsight, I was able to see the messages that movies, songs, and books are telling.

Hidden messages of the secret society and the power they have over our nation.

The fact that freedom is not free but controlled by the powerful and their will over us all.

Tolerances

Low and behold, the system is working.

With the industrial age in full swing the automobile has become the way of the world, and the creators look for ways to initiate consumption.

The formula devised by our forefathers is now fabricated to control the masses while stimulating their lust for consumerism.

Competitions are well under way, and being a man's world, gambling takes center stage.

Wagers of who will stay married and who will survive or go mad become the normal practice of the times.

What will prevail, strength or weakness?

Families begin to think of ways to ensure their family will be deemed the strongest.

Times are changing, generations are becoming larger, and people are starting to live longer.

Living longer presents a problem in competitions that last a decade.

Modern science meets ancient alchemy as a solution to that problem is devised.

Tolerances.

While some teams are allied, some are not.

Christianity remains the basis of the competition and well,

Murder is a sin.

What of poisons?

If a person built up a tolerance, they would just happen to be immune.

So that's exactly what they did.

Four poisons were chosen.

The families give their children small amounts of poisons over long periods of time.

This was and is till this day a game-changer.

With the competition becoming more and more prevalent through the generations, whole towns became an arena for the champions.

Each town chosen resembles the next.

All designed to have representatives for each family.

Strategically placing champions in areas where certain families-maintained control financially worked almost like modern assassins.

Now though if those individuals had not been raised in that area, they would not be tolerant to the substances of the other family, they were there to infiltrate.

Becoming ill and dying.

The process also worked in the opposite way if you were raised

with tolerance and your family
deemed you undeserving or no
longer felt the need to

care for you.

The substance could be removed
at which time you could become ill
and die.

Either way a testament to the
family's strength.

Evolving different chemical
tolerances which helped maintain
their power over each other's
breeding options and the areas
they fought to control.

Modern Day Eugenics.

A formula that kept family leaders in absolute control of who lived and died and when.

Forging what they thought would produce the evolved humans of the future.

In today's age, we can cure and prevent so many deaths and diseases, yet these practices are still in effect to cull the herd, per se.

Making Gods out of our family leaders who possess the gift of life or death for their people.

The decisions are based on the judgment of the shepherds herding us all like a flock of sheep.

Hand-picking who is to awaken and who is not.

Magic

For those families that were not so, tech-savvy and came from the old ways (like my mother's family),

There was magic.

The old ways granted certain powers to offset the financial aspects of the hunt, which now seems more like a game than a hunt.

Players could bet on such emotional responses of the other family's players.

All the way too, could one team's player seduce another team's husband or wife.

There was no regard to the endless possibilities of the strength test, humans could imagine to wage war.

Clenched in the thralls of a twisted game.

Magic allowed a person to speak such things into existence.

If one would only speak it out loud for all to hear, it would be made so.

This was the way of the Fae.

An ingenious way to live in poverty, while exacting such power.

The family funds locked into the collaboration of the trinity reserved for the next generation.

The creativity of the families, to indulge into their collaborative financial circles.

Now, intertwined to fund the masses, not just thirteen families.

Generations pass, children are born, families become larger and larger.

What could be worth more than money?

Power.

Power is worth more than people.

The game changes and the masses are now hives operating mostly in unison to take out the other families and secure more funds.

Everyone knows magic comes at a price,

And well gambling does too.

A scar, a tooth, an appendage,

How will you pay?

Astonishing though, magic is wonderful.

Used to better the world, the light could create miracles.

Likewise, so could the dark.

Both sides play out the consequences.

The price that the next generation would pay.

Our fate, laid out by seasoned warriors.

Hard from the strength it took them to survive, holding the pain of all the families.

Decisions are made against everything the game was created for.

Propagating slaves, born to live out the mistakes of their Elders.

Breeding, cultivating, and farming humans for the sake of the many. Prioritizing the wealth of the few.

The Titans and Gods.

Granting some magic, some beauty, and some wealth.

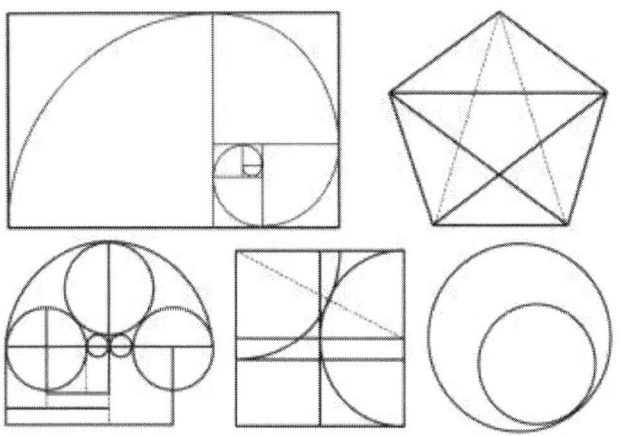

Him

So, all this societal control,
Gods and Titans.

Who knew?

Not this girl!

Stranded on the beach
heartbroken licking my wounds.

Recovering from marriage number

two.

I met Him.

His name was Tristian,

Engrossed in the hype of my
island of misfit toys.

I was having the summer of my life.

I was in better physical, mental, and emotional shape than I had been in many years.

So, I decided to live it up and have some fun.

My family was sending me to the wolves.

Why not?

And then I met him.

Consider this for a minute,

What do you think would happen if a person meets and falls in love with the opposite side's family?

Unknowingly, I was supposed to be the queen, but I had been exiled and cut off before my awakening.

HHHmmmmm....

Now let's consider for a minute,

Tristian was also destined to be his family's king but was stranded broken-hearted licking his wounds.

Living it up on a beach.

From the first minute we met, we were inseparable.

Neither one of us knew much about each other.

We began spending hours and hours talking and laughing.

Hours turn to days; days turn to months.

No one even noticed, at first.

He was a few years younger than me, and people didn't see us as, couple material, so we were Free.

I began to fall in love with him.

I was terrified and told him we can't and sent him away.

He never left, not once.

I had literally been torn to shreds by my divorce and my family thought no decent man should have me.

Unless I could still be sold to a much older man.

My looks were still good.

I was modestly pretty, and I could still fetch a price.

If I stayed unawaken, it could work.

They would wait for my fling with Tristian to be over.

Old town

We left the beach to be together and moved to Old Town.

His father had a small sailboat right on the docks and it was beautiful.

We were as poor as two people could be but the love, we shared was worth more than material things could bring.

As time went on, I almost forgot I was being hunted.

I felt as if the whole world had just melted away.

Every minute we were not working, we spent exploring the small coastal islands.

Rowing a dinghy across the creek, sunbathing and swimming.

Dancing, singing, overindulging with beer, and making love in the sun.

The rest of the world, far away, forgotten by my thoughts.

Finally, allowing my mind peace.

It was like our own little paradise.

Years go by and we decide to marry.

The shock wave of our people's reaction spreads faster than wildfire.

I was unaware of the consequences, but I can say now it wouldn't have changed a thing.

Tristian was my soulmate.

We had come from different families and different places, but we had overcome those obstacles proving,

We can all make our own destinies.

This is when I first heard the whispers.

The town was the second oldest town in America, and it was full of the graves of our ancestors.

They whispered to me as I ran amok through the small tourist town.

"We need your help", they said.

"This isn't what we intended; it's not how it's supposed to be".

"Tell everyone,"

"please".

"This is not our way".

The whispers floated through the wind.

I thought I must be crazy.

I would later find out exactly what they meant.

These whispers of the past would guide me and save my life.

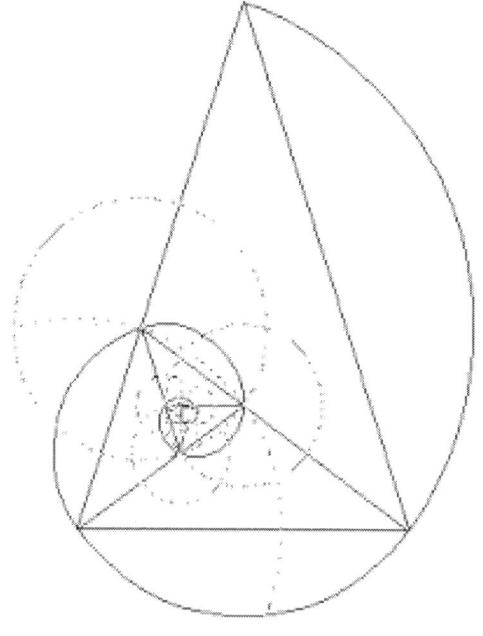

WAR

Five years go by, and America is a mess.

The opioid epidemic.

Covid pandemics.

The government is shut down and there is fighting in the streets.

Masks are now mandatory wherever you go, and the families are losing control.

The country declares war.

It was the families themselves.

Our president was a family leader and called for a Culling.

When funds ran low the family leaders would remove the tolerance of everyone.

Cycling areas with rations to keep the Essentials.

Medications are withheld and the Covid pandemic is announced.

To this day, I don't believe in the Coronavirus.

Funerals pop up on every corner, and people are literally dropping like flies.

I'm still happily married, living in LaLa land, my dad always called it.

Happy contentment with the immediate world around me

Detaching whole world problems and living a hard-earned wholesome life.

The families become manic.

They begin to count family members like dollar bills.

Assigning and reassigning attached value to each family member., Grading each member of the hunt as essential or a sacrifice for immediate funds.

All towns of masonic design will have family members from each of the original 13 families.

Each town formed into four teams' half-light and half dark.

Warriors, Gladiators of sort versed in the art of manipulation and psychological warfare.

Using the power of suggestion along with symbolism and magic to full force find and destroy members of the other houses.

Where did that leave me?

An exiled queen ghosted so that my funds would be presented to my ex-husband, remarried to a future king of his house with both teams at war.

It left me with a very large price on my head.

That's where it left me.

My family swore I was, of the dark, my husband knowing that I was not.

Six years have gone by, and no one can still agree.

The perfection of the light finds
fault in my trauma and the dark
feeds on it.

They used magic to take my looks
and tolerance to make me sick.

They found comfort in thinning
my hair, eroding my teeth, and
expanding my waist.

Like a tennis ball for two
extremes, the light and the dark.

I have been tested in every way
imaginable.

Night sweats, tremors,
headaches.

The absolute favorite method is the burn.

This process usually takes three substances, one acting as a catalyst.

Once ingested it creates a gas inside your body that blows you up like a balloon.

If you're a smoker the gas will ignite and bye-bye stomach lining.

It's really a miracle I'm alive at this point.

There is no mercy, no compassion for these families.

They have had 400 years to perfect this game in hardened souls.

People who use animals and children to hurt a person.

People who are so very far from the intentions of our ancestors who fashioned these traditions to create a society of people bound by honor, not by murder and pain.

I am strong, one of the strongest of my family.

Perks of being hunted my whole life, I guess.

Despite the situation, I chose the path of a healer.

I tell all who hunt me, that I choose to be a healer.

I chose a different path.

Designed to be a gladiator I choose peace.

Now my Quest is one of peace, a humble message to all I meet that they may hunt me, but I will walk in the footsteps of the great leaders Jesus, Buddha, Gandhi, Mother Teresa, Martin Luther King.

I am not a perfect person and that is my message.

There will always be imperfections, divisions, and things we can find to hate each other, but

we can also choose love,

I choose love.

I don't know how this will all turn out.

My family still fights to say the financial mistakes of the elders should be paid with my life.

Every day I'm inundated with poisons.

Everyday stuff no one would look for in all our foods.

Hormones to change my sex, acidic substances to change my PH, cancer-causing carcinogens in the hope they work, radiation to throw everything off balance.

The gas blows up my bowels and the oils clog my pores.

I imagine a time when society makes better choices.

When it takes personal responsibility for spreading hope and preserving life. We see our species destroying the people, animals, and life that sustains this planet.

A society of families conditioned to hunt people as if they were a sport.

Rendering most of the planet's animals extinct.

I wish I could say that it all would come to an end, that the so-called superheroes would use their magic and powers to cure and not mane, Yet the fact of the matter is, power is most important.

That's how the game works.

Money is worthless when power comes first.

Signatures

5000 signatures can buy my life.

Alright, I choose love.

I choose peace, singing it from the mountain.

Not a good idea, when you have gambling crazed perfectionists who call themselves the Light and the Dark, watching your every move.

Yikes yeah, losing the whole next generation's wealth based on their own compulsive addictions.

Consumed with winning as if they are the Gods of their families and their will is more important than the hopes and dreams of the next generations.

Losing time after time.

Whittling away at the family treasures like the poster child for Gambling Anonymous.

Sitting at a slot machine salivating every time one of those diamonds comes a little closer to the line.

Bloodshot eyes burning from the intense focus of the wheel spinning closer and closer yet always out of reach.

Greed motivates them every step while desperation erases what moral compass they had to begin with.

Supported by the hive.

Using their people as loan shark bullies in a final attempt to exalt the last drop of funds.

This is what our country now stands for,

The honor of the founding fathers reduced to freakish bullies controlling whole families' wealth in a pathetic attempt to consume more and more greed.

Their cars, houses, and toys are a testament to every person they have hunted and killed along their path to so-called greatness.

The next generation's inheritance is nothing more than poker chips thrown around on the cosmic craps table as they lose repeatedly.

Wasting every resource on pride and vengeance.

Not a good place to be singing peace and love.

I can tell you that.

My every move now was being studied.

The hive is tired from the lashing whip of their shepherds.

Their lives are consumed by the morally compromised leaders who care not of the lives of the many.

The way the system worked was once a family commenced upon a wager, signatures would need to be presented to solidify the deal.

Wagers were hence null and void if there was no third-party

involvement to validate that both parties were in fact aware of the terms and conditions. Results of such wagers, so that when a family lost their children's inheritance everyone involved would agree to the hunt.

Many times, shady backhanded arrangements and wagers were the standards for our generation, no longer a people of honor or of their word.

The family leaders use every means available to play the role of the devil,

The snake.

Tricks, and deceptions, the new way of the world.

Drugs become prevalent to entice the young.

Our elders see the young as an extension of their own lives.

The game now is a way to cheat death.

By killing off the young they could keep their assigned inheritance. But only if the young didn't make it through their awakening.

More and more young people are beginning to die.

Nothing can prepare them for the savage minds of the seasoned elders, who have spent a lifetime perfecting their wit and manipulations to use against the unsuspecting young people of our day.

How easy it was to shape their minds using the internet and marketing.

Completely unaware of the brainwashing mechanisms in place.

Systems of conformity decided before they were even adolescents if they were worthy to survive.

And there I am like snow white in a gladiator ring.

Unawaken and naive to the ways of the world.

In its simplest form, I saw it as a waste of resources for a society not far from oblivion.

Our oceans were in ruins, our forests cut down, plastic, climate change, animals in extinction, and the world's food basic crap, and this is how our families thought the world should be.

Locked in a so-called tradition that bound families in hatred and debt.

Creating slaves out of their children and grandchildren.

If not just sacrificing them for the ole mighty dollar.

Blind to the havoc of the effects on the planet.

Traditions can be a deadly thing for a species that refuses to evolve. All civilizations that fell in the past could be somehow traced to cultural beliefs and here and now we were all watching our entire planet die.

Wow.

Humanity is doomed.

Why couldn't we evolve?

Why couldn't we learn from History?

Why couldn't we use all the interconnection for positive change?

What was stopping us as a species?

Embarking on my own as a simple hairstylist to:

Be the change.

I have spent countless hours not trying to deceive or manipulate as a part of my family's so-called competition.

But to find solutions to the absolute idiocracy of our generation.

While family leaders continue to waste resources on a family game that will lead to the destruction of the planet.

A game of morality that now has no morals.

A game to find a person's moral compass by those who no longer possess one.

How have we, as a society, allowed this to happen?

The shame I feel in my heart when people come up to me and begin to speak in the language of the hunt.

My sadness is not for me but for the future generations that will be lost to an unevolved species that cares only for consumption and not for the planet that is all our homes.

The Quest

I can't say any of this has been easy, but I have learned most things that are not easy are worth it.

I know that each one of us has the capability to choose, it is and always has been the quest of the Originals.

Freedom of choice.

Free will.

What we turned it into well that was our choice too.

We allowed these family leaders and shepherds to dictate the families in this direction.

We sat back and watched the hurt, destruction, and death they created.

We closed our eyes so as not to unleash the hive on ourselves or our close loved ones.

We became the mindless sheep.

There is not a day that goes by that I don't long to be a mindless sheep again.

Free to enjoy the comforts of mundane life.

Free to live in America, the one I believed in as a child.

The one that has been the inspiration of songs, poetry, and art throughout history.

My simple standpoint is" Be the change".

Bring back the days of the golden rule and a man's word is his bond.

If our society is cursed to live out these outdated traditions let them stand for something greater than the wager of simple lives.

Let those practices inspire real choices as the governing leaders are put to the tests of the hive, reevaluating where their morality lies.

Are they men of their word?

Are they addicted to gambling with their families' futures?

Are the hunters aware of the stakes?

Is it their choice?

And when the stakes say there are no consequences then and only then can government funding gambling techniques be determined as a fair or lawful testament to what makes a man and his character.

Violent victim crimes are not the standard of men of honor wagers towards family legacies, but a new mindset that challenges become ways to better our planet or save our forest.

That the true test of family strength comes from truly changing this world for the better.

Let your family stand for something that isn't poison and death but perseverance and preservation.

Preservation of family funds for future generations and preservation of the planet we live on.

Challenge your family teams to evolve and motivate future generations to do the same.

As I awakened, I saw the power of the families, the interconnection, and the ability to work as a hive emulating the bees and animals.

Choosing those animals as their totems.

The animals and the earth, they are forgetting about in their thirst for power.

For if you are the bear, you should protect the forest and if you are the fish, you should protect the oceans and rivers and if you are of the eagle then you protect the air and the skies.

All teams coinciding coexisting to evolve our planet back to the

harmonious ecosystems that
created all our lives.

Alas, if you care not for these
things, renounce your animal
totem, and call yourself what you
really are.

The gamblers, the power-seekers,
and consumers.

Rename your families for what
they have become, not what they
have forgotten.

That when it comes to this earth,
no lives matter.

That earth's ecosystems would heal and flourish if we, the ones who keep fighting over, whose lives matter more cease to exist.

That the lives of all,

who come from all families,

should strive to rebuild all that we have taken for granted.

The planet that all the families have failed, in our lust for a game of power.

Call out to our family leaders and say:

WE WANT PEACE!

We want our planet to live, we
want to live, and we want to heal.

Call out to all families, put down
your hatred and pick up a shovel, a
hammer; rebuild.

Let our new symbols of the future
teach the next generation that we
are the ones, all of us, with the true
strength to evolve.

To say:

all lives matter,

all animal's lives matter.

and

most of all,

our planet's life matters.

Let your family's legacy of strength embrace what real fortitude is, the ability to evolve the will of a species determined to save their planet.

So that there is a next generation.

Let our elders stop their outdated ways and traditions.

becoming conscious of the horrors we would leave our people with.

A world in chaos.

Let us not be written in history as the generation who killed our planet,

But the age of action.

Collectively marking our people in all history.

I truly believe our species is there.

I close my eyes and see small communities rebuilding and reassessing their areas to what economic needs would help their people.

Stopping the hunt long enough to see what destruction it has created.

Like looking at a clear-cut lot, the trees all gone, the water all dried up.

One person notices a small flower, breaking through the clutter, the plastic, and trash.

It's as if they are seeing it for the first time.

The wreckage of our hate towards each other,

obstructing our view of what is important.

This one person deciding,

them and them alone,

could make such a difference in the small insignificant life of that one small flower.

That one action being duplicated through the community and then the state and then the nation.

That one small act of kindness multiplying like ripples across an ocean erasing the hatred that stands in its path.

The quest is to, just do today,

one small act of kindness
. If it's not for just a flower.

. Small act of kindness, the first
step in healing all of us.
We can heal our planet.
Stop hunting and start healing.
Please.
We can be the change....
I know we can.

I am

It's Easter morning, my head still
pounding, my body still shaking from
the effects of the radiation.
Blood flows from my nose.
I inform my daughter I won't be
making it.
She replies in code, there are
hunters that are out for my blood.
One a lonely old woman, looks
fading, desperate to look somewhat
like the person her mind once
resembled, now plastered with
plastic surgery.
An obsessed hunter using married
men as her prey, always being
tossed to the curb after they've had
their fill.

The other is a so-called wholesome
gentleman.
Letting his wife take the brunt of
the hunt.
Her innocent beauty is now
hardened and rugged.
They stand firm in their judgment
that they are the winners of the
game.
Using their own moral digression as
only the terms of the hunt.
Siting that their compromised
morality is only used to hunt.
Their moral compass is pure in
intentions, so that it can be used
only to find the sin in another.

That only while hunting does, one
puts the prey to the test.
They become the judge and jury.
The woman clinging to her own
sins, a mere excuse, to pardon her
behavior, over the sins of the people
she hunts.
The gentleman, firm in his decisions,
as if he would be so strong to allow
his daughter to be raped in front of
him without emotional responses.
He judges me.
That he alone would be able to
handle such consequences.
Violent victims, the calmness of
God himself.

That a person's actions are the
result of the choices of sin rather
than the empathy of many.
They judge me.
I proclaim.
Don't take my word for it.
Walk in my shoes and put yourself
to the test.
For whom pass judgment without
knowledge is weak to say.
Stand firm, it is only when the odds
are even that a man can judge.
Only when he has experienced the
tests God laid at my feet,
Could he know if his reaction
would be the same.

These hunters find life's tragic
moments a place of bets.
Yet, what of the odds if such bets
were placed on you.
That the violent crime is your child,
your love, or your heart.
Should you stand in judgment
then?
Would you remain so calm as to win
a wager?
Allowing your loved one and others
like her to be the victims of evil men
using women to fill their sexual
needs and then be killed.
Their only existence, a wet, dead,
hole for a throbbing penis.

Attached to the sorriest excuse of the male species.

Returning then, home to a wife and children.

As if he had disposed of the trash with no remorse or compassion for the women he used.

Just, prey for the hunters, weak people who deserve what they get.

A testament to a sacrifice that means nothing.

Only that your people and your families sleep well at night.

Never knowing the horrors that happen as if of no consequence, until you live through it yourself.

The woman hunts the tool of the
devil, the whore of Babylon, the
temptress,
excusing her sin to the testament of
the men she tempts, to the end, the
terms of the hunt.
Hunters have no mercy, no
compassion, and no empathy.
Just the goal, the tactic to which no
recourse shall fall on them.
Gambling all the while in a
tournament of suffering to those
who stood not to be shaken in
convictions no matter what the
stakes.

The buying and selling of human souls set out like poker chips to be exchanged at will or taken by force.
Never, I say, let the games of the hunt be that of the demons who worship it.
That beloved relationships are not torn down by their deceptions but be solidified by the faith of the righteous and the valiant.
Let all who read this remember who they are for all time.
Remember the ones who had no compassion.
The ones who had no mercy,
Let my life be the testament to those who could not forgive.

Their judgment was almighty.
Hear their words as they forsake
forgiveness.
Standing firm in their gambling
rights that my life is worth.

Remember them for all time as your
judges for when I am gone,
they will have only you to gaze their
perfection on.
That you might not be frail in your
victimization, that your decisions
during your debilitated moments are
all that anyone 's life should be
reduced to.
That all good things or kindness be
forgotten.

They are the judges, so they claim
full responsibility for their penance.
So that when you miss me or long
for my laugh or my smile or my love
for you.
You will know, it was them who said
forgiveness is above their pride.
For Jesus, himself once kissed his
betrayer as to know what judgment
would be passed.
Remember them as the judas the
ones who send me now,
to my torture,
to my death.
But no,
I will survive.

I tell myself I will overcome their
mighty fists that tie my body down
but never my mind.
Regurgitating the putrid filth of the
past.
Heaving it back into the pit of hell
for which it came.
Even so, clearing the path for the
mission at hand.
Never letting the quest out of my
wits.
Never forget the people who
needed my voice,
needed my strength,
to see there is a way.
We can all choose to be free.

Breaking the restraints of the past
and making our own destiny for a
better future.
I purge all the past from my soul.
It hurts as if it is intertwined into the
depths of my being,
but I sent it back to the people who
gave it to me.
I don't want it anymore.
It's yours, the sin seekers.
my gift to you.
I am Free.

Virtues

In the world of sin seeking hunters where were the virtues.

Seven deadly sins to test a person's character yet 12 forgotten virtues.

Would one best describe their life's existence as a result of one's virtues rather than the fortitude of his sorrow?

The things that make one's soul the description of what it means to be the light.

Should one excuse their virtues in the lust for the hunt?

Gambling their decency and honor as a mere token of their will.

Arranging much like the omnipresent pimp, the buying, and selling of the flesh.

That their virtues are merely the indulgence of their pride to convey, in an attempt, to make their egos appear mightier.

Are they then Gods of the earth in a game of depravity?

I say the challenge then is to restore human virtues as if they were the instrument of principles to which these hunters should be measured.

That the excuse of compromising another's soul much like the devil himself should be left to the demons that vanquish good and wholesome from the earth.

That the hunters be labeled as such that they resemble the charlatans, the degenerates, and the corruptors.

Making the virtues of a man his true testament of the light.

Let the dark be the seller of souls and the trickster of a man's worth

which seems no more than a wager
to make men utter slaves.

Let the words of our constitution
mean something again, restoring
faith back to the people that they
should not have to live in fear of
the so-called titans and their
wrath.

Harmonizing the division placed
upon us.

"WE the People"

that we should believe in our
leaders that they see us not as
sheep or poker chips or

unmitigated flesh but the fabric to which this country was formed.

The foundation that they need to propagate their God-like existence.

As that foundation rests on the back of the many.

The laborers, the farmers, and all the wholesome working individuals that exuberate the virtues that these titans these Shepherds lack.

Forcing them to bring our country back from the depths of hell to which it has fallen.

Healing the traditions of our ancestors which did not foresee the perversion of the hunt for future generations in a great time of possible evolution and change.

Let our time in history, then stand not as a time of misinformation but a time of great enlightenment.

Let our children and their children find means that promote virtues such as:

courage,

temperance,

liberality,

magnificence,

magnanimity,

ambition,

patience,

friendliness

truthfulness,

wit,

modesty,

and justice as their legacies upon
this earth.

That we should stop the ancestral tradition of ostracizing one of our own.

That they did not ask to be brought into this world only to suffer at the hands of the people they love and trust most.

Being sent by the families,

as nothing but prey for the hunt.

We should remove barbaric practices from a savage time in the past. Shaped now, by mature and advanced technological people.

Finding a collaborative way to instill the hunt for virtues to save this planet.

Our mother earth,

we have treated her as if she was that member of the family,

the favorite sacrifice.

We have sacrificed her to the greed of money and wealth.

We have tested her strength through sorrow,

and we have caused her to break.

Her strength crumbled like the people we forsake.

She Is weak,

losing her oceans,

riddled with debris and heat from the hunt.

The chemicals in her body make it hard to breathe.

She is losing her forests and her animals.

The poisons are killing her slowly.

We have become her cancer, and she is now put to the test.

Our test.

The test of the hunt and like so many that have not made it.

We now wonder if she will as well.

Our hunt has engulfed us all,

killing the one thing we all have in common.

While we all squabble over who is to blame.

The division's reasons to excuse ourselves from the inanimate doom facing our planet.

Refusing in every way to take
personal responsibility for our
actions.

The time is now, we have no more
excuses.

We are a species of intellectuals,
and we are evolved.

We can change the unhealthy
traditions of the past.

There is no excuse.

I say to you to lay down your hate,

and your lust for material things,

for you may not take them with
you,

when you're gone.

You find it easier to sacrifice one
of your own,

than to face your lust for
consumption.

Like an addict making excuses for
their next fix.

Giving their daughter to their
dealer as the price.

Stop your ancient ways and rise
to the future,

we can create.

The future, we are proud to leave
our children as our legacy on this
earth.

Stating,

we are the generation of change,

we are the ones who stopped the
chaos,

stopped the madness,

and remembered what is truly
important.

Our planet, our loved ones, and
our virtues.

These are the things God
created and this was his message
that he sent so many to tell.

Are we so rude as to not listen?

To be so ungrateful as to destroy
all our gifts.

Stand tall in your quest for
righteousness if you're with me.

This is my conviction,

that we can make a difference,

that we can stop the planet from
dying.

Stop the hunt and let your family
live.

Let them live as your commitment
to our mother earth.

We can heal and become whole
again.

Removing division and differences
in a common goal.

Let your victors and champions be
people of great change.

Saving our planet from the hunt
and devising ways that save us as a
species from ourselves.

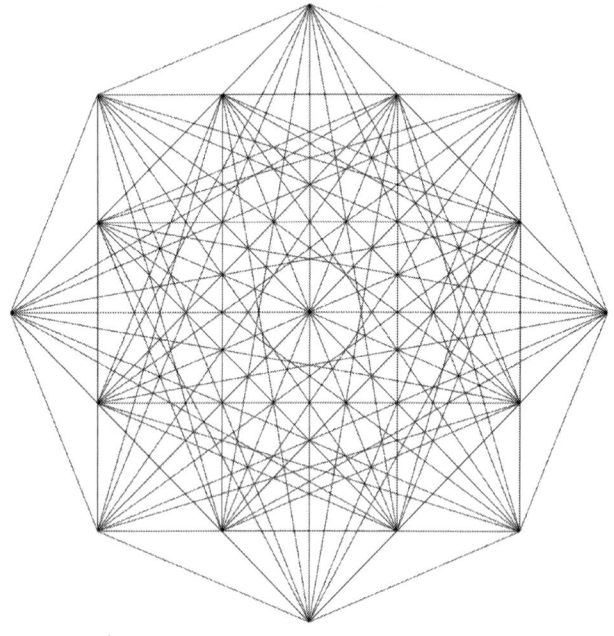

Revolution

As I walked around our new town, I could see the impact of the world changing.

I am ready to heal.

. Small gestures began to become more prevalent to the common people.

I saw people opening doors for others and picking up trash as they came across it.

The message my ancestors once whispered through the breeze, began to take shape in the actions of those around me.

The revolution had begun, and people were literally choosing to forsake the greed and corruption of the hunt and seek a better way.

A new way, our new town.

Secret and safe.

I was astonished to see the beginning of what would save our mother earth as the people themselves began to reshape our community to what was best for our planet.

Simple people first, choosing if
the directions of their materialism
would result in waste and pollution.

Growing gardens to feed their
families with non-GMO foods.

Prioritizing health as our first
common goal.

The health of our people and our
planet.

Our small community decides
what is best for their people.

We build parks and begin to see
children playing all around town.

The sound of their laughter brings smiles to even the most hardened of folks.

The children remind everyone of the task at hand,

to leave our next generation better off than the rubble of the hunt that clouded so many generations before us.

Our elders are not focused on inheritance and assigning breeding rights but are now finding ways to reverse the damage they have caused. Created by a few, an

Actor, a teacher joining everyday people to help in our cause.

Becoming our leader, education is our plan.

Next came the scientists, engineers, and farmers to aid our tasks.

The realization that the clock is ticking, and our planet and next generation need us becomes the thrill of our hunt.

Each person picks a solution to what they think they can achieve realistically.

These teams, although warring for centuries, now lay their hatred aside and begin to use that hatred as a competition to save the earth.

All of us use our totem and element as a place to begin.

Water, Air, Earth, and Fire are already divided yet now sensing the need for peace.

The teams once hungry for the blood of the hunt using their resources and skills for a new future.

This competition is the healing of our planet.

Once hunting people as prey, their loved ones as sacrifices; the sacrifices instead become the mending of old traditions and the creation of new ones.

These new traditions evolved in the quest for righteousness, not the fortitude of sorrows.

Reformulating the hope for humanity.

A list of solutions is created.

Health of the people,

Solar and alternative power,

Trash, plastic, and recycling,

Tree, bamboo, hemp, vegetation replanting, and Food.

Water cleaning and conservation are among the first priorities.

Animal and wildlife conservation.

The American dream.

America had been the place of dreams for centuries and the ability for all warring families to take pride in their country would be the glue that held the fabric together.

Still finding every reason to argue at first, the only one thing that everyone could agree on was love for our country so that was where it all had to start.

The term revolution made most people visualize something, like, the French or American revolution.

So much war and killing and violence, and the hunt had ensured that the killing would go on, but the new revolution would be silent.

We would simply walk away and while hidden, form a new place for our families to be safe.

As an evolved species the arguing had to stop the warring and the killing,

. Seeing that the families were divided into economic statuses it would have to be the crusade of these individuals to right the wrongs of the fortunate.

This country was created on the backs of the hard-working and now it would be again.

An area was selected.

A region forgotten by the establishment.

Perfect soil to start our mission,
this place, a new beginning for
humanity.

Much like Martin Luther King
using the power of love to change
the world.

We just simply grew.

Forests of food at first.

.

We turned to the advocates, the
other actors, and young people to
spread our message.

One of Love and opportunity for
change.

Separate from the fear.

The Fear.

The hunt and the instability of our nation had clamped up the flow of the economy.

It had caused a recession, a depression of sorts as our leaders placing blame, pointing fingers, and assigning faults to all in power stopped spending and started saving.

We watched from our refuge.

The government tried to stimulate the economy by sending the people checks but much like a human body, these checks were like defibrillating a dying person.

I saw, the system, as a whole, human blood not flowing to all the areas of our Establishment,

hitting that flow with CPR to try to bring it back to life.

The blood had to flow and so did the economic wealth of this country.

In order to reestablish that
economic flow,

We all had to work together, and
there again lies the problem.

In a country where every person
has three problems for each
solution,

We the common people must be
the ones to keep going to fix our
nation and create peace.

We watched from afar.

But how, how could common
people convince a political class of

warring elders to see that the
simplicity of fixing our nation was
forming alliances that propagated
change yet created harmony
between the classes.

It was better to just start again.
the area we choose, a new
beginning for us all.

We knew where change had to be
but how to get everyone on board
was the mission.

Technology was the answer.

Our nation had become a
technological powerhouse and
with the meshing of those two

worlds, we could save the world, if
we all worked together.

I saw the answers in the measuring
of happiness.

Measuring our lives.

Science, technology, engineering,
math, and agriculture are our map.

The patterns now of life, sacred
geometry our way.

It was time for the revolution to
be one of love.

"Revolution, Evolution, Love",
just like the song by Tricky, for we

all loved our country that was our commonality.

We would create the foundation to which our new traditions would reshape our country for good.

The campaign began and we had people eager for change.

Actors who spread the message of warning to our people about the damages to our planet joined our mission.

Now we were seeking to lead our people into the future.

Peace

"Imagine all the people" in the great words of John Lennon, just imagine for a minute what peace must look like.

A species in harmony with its ecosystems, and economy flowing like blood through the veins of the nation and cures for most diseases.

Can you even imagine?

Doctors that fix your body,

politicians that fix the issues,

and companies that fix our foods.

It seems like a science fiction book for sure.

Turning on the TV,

I see movies of the apocalypse.

Our humanity, first being destroyed,

before it can reach such ranks to which,

We could imagine peace.

That our only path from here to there is to blow it all up and start over again,

or to leave our planet altogether.

I shudder to think that we cannot
achieve these things.

As if, our lust for the hunt isn't as
ambitious as our race for peace.

Can we be the change, is it even
possible?

Are we evolved or is that just my
hope for us as a species?

Are we doomed to forget the
lessons of the past?

The lessons history has
documented in each fall of the
civilizations before us.

Can you see yourself as a facilitator of innovation?

These questions are the only thing stopping us from that imaginative world that we don't have to blow up to transform.

That each person alive takes personal responsibility,

to diverge steps,

to make a choice.

That we don't want to be the generation that kills our planet.

No matter what our ancestors dictated or our traditions state, that we must be wiser than the problems at hand.

What does peace look like to you?

Close your eyes and just think about it for a minute.

Can you see yourself as someone who can help achieve this path?

Can you stop hunting and start healing?

Has the pain of losing your loved ones to the hunt and the divisions our families have created?

rendered your heart cold and lifeless.

Is it that your grief and sorrow hinder your perceptions of what a world with no divisions or hate must look like?

If you were not born of such divisions, would you still hate someone among another?

Would you hunt if you were not taught to?

Back to nature versus nurture, the cycle repeats always in each generation.

It's why our ancestors designed it as such.

A repeating cycle that cannot be changed....

until we evolve.

Amida sat there in silence not believing the things he had just read.

He glared at all the people in the photos on the wall.

These were the freedom fighters. The people fighting to save our earth.

While the masses hunted and poisoned their food, water and earth these people were an interconnected network of resistance, The revolution of peace. Peace to save the planet from the formula of fear and control that had been implemented into the game of hunt.

5

"Nova, I've got to look around to see if I can find a way out." Semyon proclaimed.

Haalima spoke up. "Can you try to find Amida, please. Nova, go with him. I'll stay here with Malo."

"I always wanted a good-looking nurse." Malo grunted and grinned through the pain.

"Okay Semyon lets check out what we can."

Semyon still had the flashlight from the table, so we headed towards the back wall where Amida had previously disappeared behind the bookcases.

The resemblance of a hallway started to take shape. Covered in debris, the beams looked intact, so we began moving pieces of ceiling and earth. Clearing out the passage, piece by piece.

Hearing bumps and scrapes behind the piles of debris Amid sees a light shining through a small crevice in the heap. He jumps up to start pulling rubble to the side.

"Hey, is everyone okay?" He yells.

"I'm in here."

Excited that his friends were okay, and he would soon be rescued.

"You won't believe what I found."

"What I read."

"What I've learned."

"Nova is that you? Semyon, Haalima!"

"New Guy, whatever your name was?"

"Hey' I'm in here."

Finally, he pulled a large piece of wreckage off the top. A bright light beamed through, accompanied by Semyon's golden locks.

"Hey Semyon, I'm so glad you're, okay?"

"Is everyone, okay?" He fretted.

"Malo broke his leg. It's pretty bad. We are not going to move him till we get some help." Semyon informed Amida.

I was squeezing my way over the heap of building carnage when I glanced around the room.

"Semyon, can you help me out please?"

"Why of course my lady. Always charming, pay no mind to the dirt."

He bowed and then he softly grabbed my hands and slid me the rest of the way through the rubbish.

I dusted off my dress, pulled my hair out of my face and looked about the room.

"Amida, what is this place?" I asked intriguingly.

He was still holding the journal in his hands.

"They poisoned themselves." He blurted.

"For Sport. They poisoned the world for sport and money."

He grabbed his hair with both hands and with back against the wall began to slide down in a crouched position.

"What are you talking about Amida." I trembled.

"I don't know everything, but I was able to read this journal."

"These people in the photos. They were trying to stop the planet from being destroyed."

"There were families hunting each other for treasure, basically poisoning each other in a test of fortitude."

"They ate poison to see if they could live through it. Like for Strength."

"They poisoned the food. They did it to have things to consume, bloodlines, treasure."

"I don't know, it seems so awful.
Amida murmured.

"They hunted each other's families
for sport, each family sacrificing their
child, it's crazy."

"To be a soldier in a secret society;
A shadow government. You must
read this."

"I don't know. It is all so hard to make
out." he proclaimed.

I looked around the walls at the
faces, each one surrounded by
articles of people making tremendous
changes, effort, and real progress
trying to stop the vicious cycle.

Amida stood back up and looked at the wall and then back at me,

"These were the freedom fighters."

"They were trying to stop the food from being poisoned and save the animals and the oceans."

"Look at this one." He pointed to an article that read.

'Hollywood Actor Buys 800 Acre Bee Sanctuary in the Midwest'.

'Surfers Create Company to Clean the Ocean'.

'Farmers Finally Get to Grow Hemp'.

'Native Americans fight to keep clean Water'.

'NO-GMOS" "NO PESTICIDES'.

The articles consume the walls of everyday people, but mostly kids.

 Young people from around the world were waking up to the dangers that when their parents' generation were gone, they would be left with the aftermath. That our Elders, who could not take this wealth with them, cared more for greed and money than for the planet that provided it. Exploring space to simply leave the planet, altogether, leaving this mess to the kids of the future. The generation solely responsible for what's to come next, war or peace.

Overpopulation, World hunger, dying oceans, Animal extinction, waste accumulation, energy for the planet, the list goes on and on. These are the world problems the next generation will have to solve.

'Your generation will have to solve'. The commentary read.

The communities and small businesses and even now large corporations were trying to race the clock and heal what they had created.

A picture of a little girl in front of a podium with her hair in braids reads,

'Greta',

'Person of the Year'.

We couldn't believe our eyes.

The gardens!

There were graphical interface maps showing the damage to large areas of the planet from deforestation and aggressive agriculture. Barren lands stripped of all it had to offer, trees, soil, and animals. Nothing remained.

Documents of bodies of water polluted and animals going extinct.

Suddenly, I noticed another map. One that stood alone on the wall, with a circle of blue ink dividing a certain area.

Semyon had stopped reading and walked over to where me and Amida were standing, staring at the map.

"What is this?" He breathed while wiping the dust off the top portion of the map.

Pabulum Nation, it read in large blue writing.

The kids all stopped and looked at each other.

It was a small area that was part of a much bigger piece of land connected only by two bridges.

On the bottom of the map were the words 'Food for Thought', and there was a symbol. Our symbol, the Flower of Life.

As I peered around the room again. I started to notice them.

The symbols were scattered all around, some on the floor.

These were our symbols, our ways.

The Tree of Life.

The Seed of life.

Metatron's Cube.

The Vector Equilibrium.

They were all here, the teachings of the Divine Architect scattered around the room.

Blackboards with white writing hold formulas written out that we learn in grade school.

"What was this all about?" Semyon.

"I think these are our creators, Nova?"

"What do you mean?"

"Do you think the Divine Architect is a Man?"

"I don't know Nova, but this map. It looks kind of like the capital of Pabulum Nation, and well, it is labeled so. But I don't know what all these other lines are."

Amida Chimed in." They are states."

"The United States of America. It says it on the wall over there and in Mira's journal."

"There were fifty of them, we only have 13 provinces now. It was all part of the cleanup. We learned about that in school. "How the Divine Architect fixes their mess". Chapters 1-5. The forming of the 13 provinces."

"Guess you didn't read it yet."

"No Amida, I didn't." She grinned.

Semyon knew though. He had been allowed to study world politics after he had mastered the scholar's fundamentals. Children were taught in the discipline of the Scholars. Science, Technology, Engineering and Math along with ecological Balance and Harmony had to be learned before one could advance to world politics, economics, and social philosophy.

Semyon begins to look around the room, "Hey Amida. Do you see what that is?"

"No Way, Amida this is impossible." Shouts Semyon in excitement.

Amida turns around to see Semyon pointing his flashlight beam to the far corner.

He then looks Semyon in the face and smiles.

A large symbol of a T in an elegant curvature gleamed in the light of the beam. It stood boldly out on the back wall.

The boys looked at each other and laughed.

It was the symbol of the nation's transportation system.

An interlinked solar electric, self-driving, vehicle system networked for optimum efficiency.

There, leaned over in the corner was an early battery.

"Can You believe it." Semyon shakes his head.

"Are you thinking what I'm thinking?" asked Amida.

"You really think you can get these ancient computers working."
Laughed Semyon.

6

"So, what's up with you two anyway."
Coughed Malo.

Haalima shrugged and moved closer
to check on Malo, who was beginning
to wake up.

"Well, hey there, Handsome."
Haalima replied brushing his hair
back.

"How are you feeling Mr.?"

"I've definitely been better." He attempted to laugh, still struggling to hold back the pain.

The room is dark and dreary. Roots from the trees hang, returning the old building back to nature. A few lights remain scattered across the floor so Haalima could make out some of the wreckage. One of the archeology tables is knocked over but she can see boxes of water scattered on the ground.

"Hold on Malo, I will be right back."

She scampers around the room and comes back, lifting Malo's head to help him drink.

"I don't know what." She answers.

"We had been dating for the last two years, but things just got too hard. Choosing our career paths and all. Long story short."

"Wait, shhhh." Malo Hesitated.

"Did you hear that?"

As Haalima looked up, she could see small rocks tumbling to the ground.

The faint bark of a dog in the background.

Haalima looked at Malo and smiled.

 "Are we rescued?" She laughed.

"I sure do hope so." He replied.

The scratching and barking became louder as a puff of dust and a beam of light saturated the room from above.

"Helloooo." A familiar voice echoed through the room.

"Mr. Norman, It's me, Haalima." She shouted.

"All of us are down here. Please. Help!"

The dog barked in excitement at his discovery.

"Okay kids, I'm here but, I must go get help to get this rubble removed and I need another ladder tall enough to get down to you."

"Bring a doctor, please." She shouted. "Malo is Hurt."

"Okay kids." He yelled. "Hold on tight, we're going to get you out of here safely."

A moment of peace came over them both but what of their friends?

"Should I try to go find them?" Asked Haalima.

"No Haalima, I don't want anything to happen to you. Wait for Mr. Norman."

7

Nova dusts off the monitors and the boys lift the T battery back up against the wall.

"It must have a solar storage tank on here somewhere." Amida beamed with excitement.

"Theoretically, it could have kept energy stored even till now if it was sealed. It may just need a spark to kick the operating system back on."

"These flashlight batteries are made by the same company."

He opened the back of the flashlight and took out the battery stem card combo. The same shiny T emblem engraved into the metal.

He then ripped the wires out of the rest of the flashlight.

The room went dark.

As our eyes adjusted the boys fiddled around until lifting open the network manual operating box and connecting the two wires.

"Cross your fingers." Malo cringes and pushes the button.

Nothing.

A unison sigh filled the room.

"I don't understand! It should work." Groans Amida.

"I want to get us out of here."

He yells loudly and kicks the machine.

A blast of light fills the room. Somehow, the entire system kicks on and the sound of the monitors uploading, lights buzzing and old-fashioned music playing stuns us all.

Amida runs to the computers and sits down.

His curiosity peaked.

"Okay! These are the keyboards." He held up what, I assumed, was more plastic, a device with letters.

"This is kind of like ours." He gleamed.

"I think I can get this one back online."

Clicking away, on a black screen with green letters, he hacked into the hard drive.

The screen displayed a slideshow of pictures of a place. Land where people were not fighting at all or wearing masks. The pictures showed groups of people planting trees, bamboo, and hemp, the land still barren in the background progressing to photos of forested lush vegetation.

A community working together, simply growing, and installing early solar panels to harness the sun.

This community seemed different just from the appearance of their smiles and the way their eyes gleamed.

Hard work, ambition, and joy exuberating in the photos with food and vegetation all around.

The three of us were engrossed by the images on the screen of ancient people fighting for what was right. The freedom to eat food with nutrients, drink clean water and not pollute the planet. Their American Dream. Raising their families free from the hunt.

Pure, growing for their people and planet.

We could see how truly happy it made them.

Possibly, the same feeling we experienced for the harvests.

A feeling of accomplishment that satisfies the soul. The cycle of life, feeding our people but still replenishing the earth. Preserving for future generations the planet that provides for us all, with Balance and Harmony.

Amida navigates the files and comes across a video.

It's the same man in the pictures and articles on the wall.

The video is a documentary to educate the masses on the destruction they were creating. Warnings to all the people of that time that they had to: Be the Change. If our species was to survive.

A file named Pabulum Nation scrolls across the screen.

We looked at each other puzzledly and opened it.

The same map as on the wall is now on the screen in front of us. A semi secluded land mass area quarantined off from the rest of the region by means of the Coronavirus. Forgotten by most but perfect soil for others.

Someone had divided the area into a plausible plan for community, power, water, and Wi-Fi grids. Separating from the interconnected framework of the masses and drawing by hand new systems of operation. Pictures of cars with the same T emblem displayed next to new plans for roads.

Amida clicked on diagrams of hydroelectric generators and windmills of all forms.

The plans were immense, each one connected to the symbols of the Divine Architect as an outline of design.

It was so confusing how our ways were intertwined in their designs. The dark ages were decades of greed and corruption, our teachers said, and would not teach it. How then were these symbols engraved into the substance of the people who lined the walls. I looked back up at all the faces.

Were these our predecessors?

Amida, still going through the Pabulum Nation files, pulls up a photo.

The advertisement read.

Be the Change.

Pablumnation.com

Under it a list of individuals and companies, who were embarking on a new way of life. These people had joined together under the direction of this site to form what they called 'Green Cities'. A place where the freedom fighters could turn their backs on the unhealthy traditions of the past and begin to cultivate and evolve free from the chaos.

Pabulum Nation was their sanctuary.

Free from plastics, GMOs, and pesticides, the rest of the world was drowning in.

The photos on the main screen, the Originals. The first of their kind to want something different for their children and their planet.

Unorganized and cluttered, the photos told a story of people unsure and apprehensive of the choice to change yet becoming more confident and skilled as time progressed.

Semyon notices a file that is blank, although it is saved as multimedia.

"Amida pull this file up, will you?"

"Sure." Amida answers.

It was a video log. Recorded video conversations between this new settlement and this computer established as the command center. Separated from the existing systems, the library was the only outside connection. A central database of likeminded individuals relying on each other as a network for innovation. From what we could make out, the primitive science of their time was the fundamentals of our ways. Starting from the grade school concepts of our people, they discovered the commonality of the Divine Architect as the pattern of Harmony and Balance. Finally, they had woken up just like Mr. Norman had stated. The Great Awakening. This was the moment life on the planet changed and we were standing right in front of it.

Amida pushed the first video log, and it was the man from before.

Pabulum Nation: November 10th, 2021.

"How's it going Leo?"

"Great Woody. I met with a group of scientists last week and we think we have the solar battery issues figured out. This headquarters is fully solar as we speak." Leo Confided with a smile.

"I think they were actors." Semyon interrupted.

"Look at the pictures over there," and he pointed.

A group of people in the photo, smiling with a sign that read 'Go Green'.

Then another,

'Hollywood actors use their influence on Climate Change Advocacy'.

"Did you get the bamboo and hemp forest planted?" Leo asked.

"The community has been working on it all week. I'm super stoked to see the progress. The farmers have been a tremendous help."

"Did you get the photos I sent?" Woody questioned.

"Yes, I uploaded them to the website. We literally have had 175,000 hits since yesterday." Leo's excitement is apparent in this voice.

"How is Mira? And Tristian?" He asked.

"Mira is recovering. We have managed to get most of the poison out of her system and well we have fresh food growing every day, it won't be long before she's back to her old self again." He laughed.

"Great." Said Leo.

"Well, tell her and the others it's working, if we can just keep things on the down low for a little while longer. I think the amendment to let Arnold run for president is going to get passed. It's been a Hella fight, but if anyone deserves to be president, so that this country can heal, it's Arnold. Did I tell you he has picked Shaq as his running mate?"

"Keep your fingers crossed." Leo held up his fingers crossed.

"Soon, we won't have to hide the amazing paradise we all have created for the world, any longer."

"Just, gotta shift the powers that be, and hopefully that will slow down the climate crisis fast enough to stop the destruction."

"Awesome Leo, things here are evolving nicely."

"If you can send us the stats on those roadways from Elon, that would be great."

"Just email them to us." Woody smiled as he began to turn the camera.

"Check this out Leo." The scene swooshed around to the most beautiful garden of bamboo, hemp, fresh vegetables, and flowers. Lined by numerous kinds of fruit trees.

"Whatcha think?" He laughed as the camera swooshed back to him.

"It's beautiful." Leo remarked.

"How are Morgan's bees?"

"Dude, the honey is Divine..." Woody laughed.

"The wife and I will send some in the next shipment for you. Oh yeah and tell Jane the animals are adjusting well."

"Thanks man, till our next transmission take care." And the video log went blank.

Standing there in awe, we looked at each other.

We had witnessed history in the making. The beginning of a new way of life for our planet and our humanity. The only reason we were standing here today.

As Amida scrolled through the video logs, the progress was phenomenal in a short amount of time. It's truly amazing what our species can achieve when we all work together for peace. The rise and fall of civilizations before achieving greatness, then destruction, the human legacy. Until that moment.

The moment when finally, our species decided not to fall, but to change the path of destruction to one of peace.

We kept scrolling, thinking how wonderful this all was when we came across something different. These videos were groups of angry people. The cities were getting worse. The culling and the hunters targeting people who were trying to change. Families trying to break free of the unhealthy traditions and heal. Growing fresh food, collecting rainwater, and teaching their children peace not war. Men in masks consume the videos controlling the masses with fear.

Corporations fight to maintain their power. Plastic companies are unwilling to look to composites from plants rather than fossil fuels. Resistant to change based on their pride and money.

These companies hire teams of attorneys. The people in the videos plead with the Establishment to open their eyes and stop polluting the earth.

We scrolled through and watched as many as we could during the time we were there. Stories of how they had kept the region a secret from the mainstream. Growing four seasons before accidentally being detected.

Apparently, A local older woman, Yazmin, was returning from Pabulum to her home across the river by boat, when she was apprehended by the authorities. Her boat was teeming with hemp, food, fresh fish, and water. The mainstream, while still controlled by fear, were hungry and sick. Although, in trouble from the hemp, the crowd demanded to know where the food was coming from, and Yazmin was refusing to tell. A team of lawyers cross examine her in court. Threatening to take her house and throw her in jail.

The people of Pabulum who had forgotten the fear, begin to worry and stress over what they should do.

What would happen if the Hunters found them? The establishment is corrupt and full of greed. The people of Pabulum study the ways of the earth as their source of freedom.

"I'll go." Informed Woody.

"I'll go talk to them to see if I can get her set free."

The group turned to his guidance, as their community's builder. Creating a refuge for all.

"What will you say?" asked Tristian.

"I'll invite them to come." Explained Woody.

"Here, to our Sanctuary." Yelped Tristian.

Leo silent in contemplation.

"No, you can't, you just can't bring them here."

"All our hard work, Woody, no, please." A group of voices from behind the camera objected in fear.

Leo spoke up. "I think I'll get ahold of Arnold to see if he can help."

"It's the only way, to let them see." Woody shook his head and stopped filming.

8

In the distance Haalima hears the faint bark of a dog.

"He's back." She spoke. Running her fingers through Malo's hair to gently wake him, so happy to hear people approaching.

"Kidssss." Yelled Mr. Norman. His voice echoed.

"Yeah, we're still down here, Mr. Norman."

"Helloooo." Hollered Nova's Avus.

Just as the beams of light entered the room, the end of a tall ladder was being shoved down the hole in the roof.

Haalima could now see Mr. Norman's boots stepping down the ladder one by one, with several other beams of light bouncing about from up above.

"Malo, they are here. We're going to get you help." She assured him.

"Mr. Norman, did you bring the doctor? Malo's leg is broken."

She had moved to the bottom of the steps as Mr. Norman reached the floor.

"Yes Haalima. What in the world happened?"

"Where are the others?" he asked, scratching his head as he looked around.

"We came down here to find Amida. She stated that when the bookshelf fell, Nova and Semyon went to find Amida and Malo's leg."

"I stayed to help him." She rambled.

"Slow down Haalima. It's all okay. I thought the dig was secure. Amida was so curious I should have listened when he was questioning me about the site. That kid is so impulsive."

Two other men were making their way down the ladder with a gurney.

"We're going to get you out of here, Malo."

"Hang tight." Mr. Norman said as he was gently lifting the torn dress bandage and assessing the damage.

"Ouch." He flinched as he looked at Malo cringing.

"Oh, it's okay." Said Malo. "I've had the best nurse ever," and he looked at Haalima, wincing a grin.

The two men came over with their bags, "I'll be okay Haalima." Malo directed.

"Go find the others."

Mr. Norman pried Haalima away from Malo. And the two of them started making their way towards the shadows, where the others had disappeared. Haalima glanced back to see Malo being lifted on the stretcher.

As they rounded what was left of the bookshelves, they were surprised to hear the muffled sound of music. A light was glowing from the top of the heap of rubble. Haalima and Mr. Norman looked at each other confused.

"Nova, are you in there?" Haalima yelled.

"Amida? Mr. Norman is here."

Mr. Norman had started climbing through the hole, but he was much larger than the kids, so he found himself stuck.

Semyon, noticing the rocks falling from the other side, stops and runs over to help.

"Watch out, Haalima." Mr. Norman warns from above. She can only see the back half of his body. Legs kicking as he tries to force himself though.

Semyon climbs up to the other side and sees Mr. Norman's head.

"Well, hello there." Mr. Norman replies.

"I would guess that you are Semyon." He chuckled as Semyon reached around pulling debris out of the way to help Mr. Norman make more room.

"Yes sir, I am he." Answered Semyon.

"Are the others with you?" He asked.

"Yes, sir they are."

"Great." Mr. Norman replied. "Haalima is right on the other side."

Semyon grabbed Mr. Norman's hands and pulled with all his might as he wedged the rest of the way through.

"Can you be so kind as to get Haalima through safely, Semyon?"

"Yes sir." Affirmed Semyon and through the crevice he went.

Mr. Noman looked around the room.

Amida stopped scrolling through the files and looked up from behind the screens with a meek gesture as to assess Mr. Norman's mood.

He carefully slipped the journal into his back pocket without detection.

"Nova, go help Semyon get Haalima please." Grumbled Mr. Norman as he took out his handkerchief to wipe the dirt off his face.

"How did you get these ancient lights and computers to work?" He queried.

Looking sternly but inquisitively at the same time.

Amida pointed to the system's battery on the back wall, still unsure what to say.

Semyon and I walk over to the desk and all of us are standing in front of the ancient computers.

"Did you tell him what you found, Amida?" asked Semyon.

"What did you find, repeated Haalima?"

"How is Malo?" I asked.

"He is good, they are helping him out as we speak." She responded.

Mr. Norman is looking around the room with the same awe the kids experienced upon their arrival. Scratching his head, he absorbs as much information as he can.

"Did you kids see all this, oh my Divine Architect." He whispered as he walked slowly head cocked to the side to read as many articles as possible.

"Mr. Norman, ahhh, we have videos. Here on the computer." Amida interjected, still nervous about how much trouble he was going to be in.

"You really did it then." He chuckled.

"You got these ancient systems up and running?"

"Yes sir, I did, only because someone in the past had thought ahead to set the system up. The containment system was still preserved all this time. Seeing that it was one of our primitive technologies I was able to basically jump start it."

"The Divine Architect, Pabulum Nation." Semyon and I both blurted out at the same time.

"Whoa kids, one at a time." Mr. Norman was still engrossed in the information scared around the room.

"We found the beginning, Mr. Norman." We directed Mr. Norman to the computer screen.

The video on the screen media coverage of Yazmin's trial. The crowds outside surround the courthouse with droves of people holding signs.

'Free Yazmin for the planet!'

'Save the bees!'

'Food without GMOS!'

'No More Plastic!'

'No More Culling!'

The crowd was divided into those wearing masks and suits.

Mr. Norman's mouth is wide open to the shock of the images in front of him. We intensely watch as Woody walks through the large assembly, bombarded by reporters, to make his way into the courthouse.

As he walks into the building the video skips and we are unsure of what is happening inside the trial.

The very next log entry shows a very excited Woody talking with Leo about how he had made some progress in inviting the entire judicial faction along with certain members of the media to a guided tour of the sanctuary they had created on the condition they let Yazmin go.

Pabulum Nation is announced for the world to see.

"Did you get a hold of Arnold?" He asked Leo.

"Not yet, He was on campaign. I left a message with his secretary explaining everything that was happening here. And for him to contact us as soon as he can. Running for president is no easy task, he will be in contact as soon as he can."

"When is the meeting?" asked Leo.

"It is three days from now," said Woody.

"Good luck, Woody. If they would lift the travel ban. You know I'd be there."

Mr. Norman is glowing with excitement again. "WOW." He chattered.

"We must go kids. Nova your Avus is up there waiting worried sick about you."

"Mr. Norman, we must see what happens, please." We all gasp and groan.

The kids were in absolute suspense for the next video to what may have happened to these people who had created Pabulum Nation.

We could hear people behind the mound of debris. "Are you in there, are you okay?"

"Yes." Replied Mr. Norman.

"We are okay."

"We need to get all you out of here. We have assessed the damage, and it is not safe." Yelled a strong male voice from what was left of the hallway.

The kids looked at each other and then back at Mr. Norman. "Please Mr.

Norman." Amida begs. "We must know what happens next."

"We have to know." Semyon interjects.

I look at Haalima and her facial expression pleading. "We must know, please just a few more minutes."

"We are safe." Yells Mr. Norman to the man.

"We will be right out. Give us just a few minutes."

Mr. Norman, himself curious, turns to Amida and smiles.

"Hurry let's see what their last video log says and then we must go." Amida pushes the file, and they all look towards the screen in full concentration.

9

"Good morning and welcome to Channel 8 News."

  An attractive lady popped up on the screen.

"Today we will be touring Pabulum Nation. A region of land once quarantined from the mainland by means of the Coronavirus, Now transformed by likeminded individuals and businesses to be what they call the city of the future."

"I'm standing here with one of those individuals, who has agreed to let both the media, law enforcement and the court's view what many are calling a Hippie Cult."

Woody looks down, shakes his head, and laughs.

"First of all, I'd like to start by saying, we are not a Hippie Cult. We are an Agricultural Cooperative belief network redesigning what our vision of the future should look like. Using science, technology, engineering, and math in reference to the sacred geometry of the earth. Thus, preserving our ecosystems. Reversing climate change so, basically being in harmony with our planet."

"Our sanctuary is a well-educated hypothesis of what would happen if all individuals took personal responsibility for the planet they live on."

The Media, Judges and Police begin to look around while Woody and the other people of the community join in

to show the world what they have
created.

Mira and Tristian direct a group to
the permaculture forest. This garden
is for Greta, a sign read. Apple and
plum trees stick out from the grove,
but as the eyes wander the woods
are alive with grapes, blackberries,
figs, and pears. Mushrooms, peanuts,
and strawberries Every Fruit tree a
person could imagine growing free in
abundance.

Rows of vegetables and flowers are
immensely beautiful as they grow in
harmony with the environment. The
aromas of garlic, onion, marigold,

basil, lemongrass, fennel, and dill linger in the breeze.

There are hemp and bamboo forests that are soaring tall and strong, removing carbon from the atmosphere, and returning it to the earth. Cotton fields resemble a dusting of snow. These plants are used for textiles such as clothing, linens, toilet paper, and rope. The number of products that can be made are countless. One of the girls from Pabulum shared.

The group is in awe of what they see in front of them, and a few begin to remove their masks as they make their way to the town center.

The community's homes reveal themselves.

The homes were fully green, electric by means of solar, hydro, and turbine power. Working in unison to supply free clean energy to all that lived there. These homes are optimized to conserve as much power as possible. Each structure operates as a local business and house. Showcasing each person's unique contribution to the community.

Tristian explains how the toilets are all compost so that they maintain the fields and their gardens. Water is supplied from an aquifer filtered fresh and clean.

These homes were modern and equipped with technology to stay in balance with their ecosystem yet just as nice, clean, and lavish as the outside world.

As more and more of the guests begin to remove their masks, the group walks into the central courtyard.

"We are still constructing this area." Woody spoke up.

"It will include a spiritual garden where people can pay respects to whichever religions they practice. This way, all that live here can coexist in harmony yet, still work towards our common goal of preserving the planet for future generations."

"The area to the right is the outdoor kitchens and central dance floor. These areas are for town festivals and times of celebration focusing on art, music, and philosophy."

"But, Ladies and Gentlemen, the crowning jewel of our city is our transportation system."

One of the community members pulled up in a crude version of the vehicles we drive today.

Woody explains. "We are in the process of building our transportation system for our people."

"It will be a self-driving optimized electric transportation system that everyone can access to stay in exact harmony with carbon emissions, thus saving the planet from its addiction to fossil fuels. You can see here, the system will include roads that are light in color and surrounded by trees to keep the planet cool, while still meeting the needs of those who use it. We are planning to have this finished in approximately one year." He turned to Tristian in agreement.

"Yes." Tristian said. "We hope to be finished by the beginning of the next harvest."

"This addition will conclude our city's ability to be a functioning green city providing food, water, energy, and housing to the people who live here, while most importantly, reducing the carbon imprint on the planet. In conclusion, we will be able to reverse the effects of the climate crisis leaving the planet free from pollution and waste in a very short amount of time."

"Excuse me." The District Attorney blurted out.

"Yes?" Woody replied.

"So, how does the economic system work? Money?"

"Well, we operate on credits. He explained. Each person, basically, bartering for material possessions they want rather than need. The things we need to survive are provided by the system, so that each purchase made will be thought out as to how it will reflect on the planet or how it will be disposed of after its use."

"What about jobs?" Someone yelled from the back.

"Our jobs are as such, we must work together." Woody conjected.

"No jobs, no money, how is this possible?"

"Our city is based on education." He explained. "Look we haven't worked out everything, yet this is a group project. We have farmers, engineers, scientists, computer scientists and everyday people working together to be free from the constraints of the world you live in."

"Working nonstop to find a better way. Free from the hunt, the culling, and the virus."

"We are doing it. Look around people." He bellowed. "Can't you see we're doing it to save the world."

"Look at this place, there is no sickness, no greed, no culling, just people learning to live in harmony with the planet."

"I've seen enough." Judge Powe roared. "These people are under arrest."

The news lady grabs her cameraman to get every bit of the arrest on video.

"I declare that everyone here is in numerous violations of every ordinance there is in the law books. Do you have any ideas, the fines alone?"

He signals the police officers to put back on their masks, and then commands. "Every single person here is to be arrested, Until I can decide how to prosecute them."

"There have been no permits, no inspections, you have not registered this hemp with the dept of agriculture. Building homes, power and water systems, my God, I can't even begin to list the charges every one of you are facing." He shouted from beneath his mask.

The officers look at each other shocked and confused. The freedom they were witnessing was a testament to all that they swore to protect.

All the while, the cameraman filmed as the community members shrieked in fear.

Mira runs to Tristian shaking, the memories of being hunted still fresh in her mind.

He grabs her and holds her close as the police begin to come closer. Each person wide eyed and suspenseful of what is going to happen when the first set of handcuffs are exposed.

At that moment Woody jumps on the table and faces the group of law enforcement.

With a loud cry, he yelled.

"This is our home, and we will not live-in fear."

"You are our guests, and you will be treated as such, but there will be no arrests."

"Not today or any day."

"This is Pabulum Nation, and we are free."

He looked at his people.

"We will not live-in fear." He Swore.

Judge Powe's anger steamed from his face as he looked at the police. They were torn on what to do. Each one armed and ready to fulfil the obligations to their jobs yet now aware that change and happiness without fear was possible.

"Do your jobs." He commanded them.

"Arrest these individuals, they are breaking every law there is or so help me God, I will have your badge."

One officer takes out his gun hesitantly, and then another. The crying people of Pabulum, unarmed and peaceful, begin to scatter and hide.

Woody stands firm in his decision to protect his people, and Judge Powe stern in his penance.

10

Without warning, a loud turbulence encompassed the sky. The pandemonium adds to the terrifying hostility of what actions the armed men will take against the community.

As the camera looks up, we can see the legs of a helicopter attempting to land as fast as possible. The roaring of the blades pushed wind down on the officers causing them to cover their heads and retreat. Judge Powe and the DA running with them.

Woody is still standing on the table. As the chopper sets down to land, Leo and another man jump out. The man with him is holding a briefcase. And they start to run covering their heads towards Woody.

"We did it." Leo said. Woody climbs down from the table and walks towards Leo turning his back to the wind.

The news camera now focuses on the men.

"We did it." Leo yells and laughs.

"Meet our Lawyer." Leo pats the young man on the chest.

"What did you do Leo?" Woody was confused yet so very happy to see him.

"Not me." He laughs. "We, We!"

"Diplomatic Immunity." The Austrian accents asserted from behind him.

Woody's face grinned from ear to ear as he turned around with sheer excitement.

"Arnold, Catch my friend."

Woody throws an apple from the table.

Arnold catches the apple in midair, smiling and then takes a bite.

"That's President Arnold to you." He smiled.

"I've granted this region to the Pabulum Nation. Your very own Providence. You and the people of course."

"We the People!" Woody grabbed Arnold and hugged him.

The Establishment was being ushered away.

The news reporter then faced the camera again. She was crying and laughing all at the same time.

"This is Harper Whitlock Channel 8 news, and this is history in the making." The camera then went blank.

We all just stood there in silence. As we looked at each other, tears flowed down our cheeks and the happiness filled our hearts, this was history, she was right. Our history.

Mr. Norman let out a sigh, we were looking at the freedom fighters that paved the path to our world. The Divine Architects, all of them.

They had fought to build a new world and we were standing in that world today. This world was brought into reality as the direct result of the actions of people working together to find a way. Clean and fresh. Not governed by power, money, or things but for the one true thing they all had in common. Our earth.

11

"Mr. Norman?" A voice shouted from the other side of the rubble.

"We must get you all out of here now." The voice was full of alarm. "Please."

Mr. Norman turned to us.

 "Let's get out of here." He concurred.

We looked around one more time to burn the images in our minds forever.

Haalima went first over the mound of debris, the man on the other side helping her through. The panic apparent in our every move. Scurrying as fast as we could.

Semyon insisted I was to go next. He smiled and helped me over. As my eyes adjusted to the dark, I stood there waiting for him patiently. The creeks of the ancient building began to moan.

"Hurry Semyon." Uttered Amida. He was squeezing his way through but all we could see was the top of Mr. Norman's head.

"Hurry Mr. Norman please, we must get out of here." I yelled.

The men who were there pulled us away as we looked back.

Mr. Norman was nowhere in sight.

"Amida, where is Mr. Norman?" Semyon wailed.

The creeks and moans rang out louder this time.

The men were forcing me up the ladder, pulling on my arm as I yanked to get free.

Semyon, fighting, and kicking, trying to see where Mr. Norman was.

"We can't leave him." He screamed.

Amida breaks free from the man and as fast as he can, runs back to the hallway where Mr. Norman was last seen.

"Mr. Norman, where are you?" He cried. Attempting to crawl back over the heap just as a man grabs his clothes and pulls him back.

"We are not leaving him." Amida screams.

The man grabbed him by the waist, picked him up off his feet, and threw Amida over his shoulder and headed towards the ladder.

My eyes searched and searched the ground as I made my way back up the ladder as fast as I could. A line of people behind me pushing me to hasten every step.

As I step onto solid ground, I turn back to see the boys one at a time exiting the void. The men who were there to help evacuate the area, still shoving us out of the direct path of the dig site.

"Where is Mr. Norman?"

Our eyes look at each other in despair as a long moaning bellow rises from the ground. The sounds of wood cracking echoed through the forest as we all stood there in trepidation.

I couldn't look, I shielded my eyes in Semyon's chest, warm and safe as my imagination feared the worst. A moment goes by, and we all hear the blast.

Looking up I see a hand on the rung of the ladder still standing firm in the hole. Then, another hand comes into view, this one holding tightly a photo from off the wall.

"Mr. Norman." We yell, as he climbs out huffing, falling on his back in exhaustion on the solid ground.

The tears fell down my face again, our teacher safe. The men from before rush over to help him up and out of the way just as the ground around the ladder starts to give way.

There is a tremendous crash. Dust engulfs the air making it hard to breathe and the library is gone. Swallowed by the earth. The entire dig site is now a crater of earth and debris.

Cradled in Semyon's arms, the magnitude of the situation hits me. My legs feel weak, my body is trembling. He softly runs his hands through my hair, and I feel safe. As I gaze up to look in his eyes, he tenderly grabs my chin and kisses me. It's as if the horrors of this day vanished, the muffled sounds of panic in the background disappearing in that very moment.

I am free.

12

"Malo, get back here."

 "You cannot race that hoverchair through the halls." A plump nurse scolded as she scampered to catch up to Malo.

"Are you kidding?" He laughed.

"My friends are here to break me out of this place." Malo laughed as he gravitated as fast as he could so that the nurse could not catch him.

"Malo, give the lady a break." Semyon shook his head and tried not to laugh.

"Tell her to get me my robotic brace, so I can break free from here." Malo stopped to let the nurse catch up and direct him to his room.

"Dear Divine Architect." She fumed as she pushed the chair back into the hospital room.

"Your dismissal will be here any minute." She replied. "I'll go get your things and she promptly exited the room."

"Nova, have you spoken with Haalima?" Malo asked. "Will she be there today?"

"Of course, she will be there, we are all going."

"Mr. Norman wants us all to be there."

"Oh, so Amida will be there too." Malo squinted his face to make a funny grimace.

"I thought you two talked about this already, Malo."

I comforted him.

"Amida is leaving next week for the western provinces. He will be gone for two years and although they will always care about each other, she chooses you, silly."

"You're going to make a fantastic farmer Malo." Semyon chimed in. "Now let's get out of this place."

The Nurse was walking back into the room with Malo's robotic brace. She placed the brace around his leg, and he immediately jumped up.

"I'm free." He laughed, "now let's get out here." Malo was excited as a schoolboy to be on the way to the Gardens of Greta. Although he had recovered quickly from the dig, the injuries had cost him his place in the Nation's Guard. A position he was happy to trade to be with Haalima.

"What time are we supposed to meet her there." He asked.

"She is meeting us there in an hour Malo." I grinned.

Semyon pulled me closer to him as we rode. I loved being close to him.

The vehicle stopped and standing at the gates of the Garden were Mr. Norman, Amida, and Haalima.

Malo and Haalima were grinning from ear to ear yet trying to be cool as Mr. Norman shook Malo and Semyon's hands.

"Glad to see you boys again."

"Hello Nova. Hello Amida. Hello Haalima, Hello Mr. Norman."

"Hey Malo, Semyon."

We all made our salutations and then walked to the center of the Garden.

13

Everyone's energy felt solemn as we approached the statue of the Divine Architect in the central courtyard. We were so lucky to be alive, a feeling that overtook us, as we looked at each other and joined hands.

Mr. Norman took the picture he had saved from the command center out of his vest pocket. As we looked at all the faces in the picture, the emotions of what we had experienced came over us. These were the Heroes of the past. The freedom fighters who forged our world, and we were here to pay our respects and then never speak of this again.

The knowledge that our greatest achievements were formed by men and women like us would be too much for this era to bare. That the Divine Architect of the future needed to stay as we all remembered him to keep the Balance and Harmony of our ways. This divination, the sacrifices these individuals made, created our society as one that honored and cherished the ecosystems of our Earth. Designing ways of unity for humanity, now evolved. Our legacy, preserving the actions these individuals took to overcome the odds and harness their reality. Keeping them always in our thoughts but sealing their memories in our hearts forever. Our world, the direct result of their perseverance. Mr. Norman passed around the picture.

We looked at it one more time to burn the image in our mind forever. Then he set it on fire. The flames burned green, blue, and orange consuming the faces of the past. He dropped the photo engulfed by flames on the ground at the base of the statue. We watched as the very last part of the paper turned to ash.

They were free.

This book is dedicated to my family...

In hope that we can create a better world.
Love you, Kristian,

Love you Parents and Sister,

Love you Kids...

Hailey

Savannah

Logan

Vera and Avie

Be the Change!

Rachel Barron Schurdevin

Aka
Nova Schurdein

Exert from my next book coming out soon....

Ughhh! I felt as if my whole body was on fire. Ughh. My eyes slowly peeled open as if they were never open at all.

My body. MY BODY! Oh, my. It is here, it was attached.

I slowly felt my hands, my legs, they were here.

My eyes peeled open again and yet I could not yet make out where I was.

As I felt, along my body, the blankets were soft and there were tubes and things that pulled the skin on my hand as my hands made their way across my body. How is this possible. My body is still here. I am alive.

I tried to speak the words would not come out. Just utters of syllables that tried to flow from my mouth yet only blurts of whispers that didn't make since.

I still felt so dizzy, and the room was bright and cold.

I felt my lips, they were dry, my face still there but cold and placid.

What and where was I?

The confusion filled my mind.

I searched my thoughts for something anything that could make since.

I could still hear the screams of the crowd. The smell of the mob. My hands. The little fingers of my children. My husband led in front of me. As I watched him being led to his death.

The slamming of the guillotine brackets around my head.

My head! It's still here.

I felt the bandages on my neck as I lay there still trying to feel my body. Forcing it to wake from what felt like an endless slumber.

I reached my hand out to what looked like a table next to me. The table filled with flowers and a glass. I reached for the glass of water using all my might but as I did it fell to the floor, and I could hear the crash echoing through the room into what seemed to be a hall.

A woman came running in, her clothing nothing like I had ever seen before.

The panic came over me and I tried to scream. The scream muttered into the crackle of my voice. Horse and squeak.

The woman rushed over to me and hit a button on the wall.

"Code Blue, Code blue" The nurse yelled.

As I see her pull out something from her pocket.

I kick and scream.

The tubes pull from my hands as two more women enters the room to hold me.

Où sont mes enfants!

The words finally coming from my mouth just as a needle from one woman hits my leg.

I kick one more time, knocking her back into the wall as I feel the heaviness come over me.

I close my eyes and I am gone.

"Well, that was crazy."

The nurses turned to each other and laid the woman back down on her bed.

Blood from her IV had seeped onto the bed and the room was a mess.

"Can you believe she woke up?" She's so beautiful, I thought she'd never wake." The cheerful nurse went about straightening the woman's hair and returning her back to a comfortable position.

"I can't believe she woke up with that wound around her neck. I thought she'd stay in a coma forever.

Did the report say what it was from?" The nurses chattered about as they tidied up.

"No one knows. She was found floating in the river down by the old ports. Nothing but an antique night gown. Some very expensive earrings and a priceless antique wedding ring. The cops took everything to the evidence locker. No one knows where she came from, who she is or how she got there. And especially the wound that goes all the way around her neck."

"Geezz, she should be most fortunate that she didn't lose her head. Did you see that scar."

The nurse unwrapped the bandages around the woman's neck. A bright pink scar in a perfect circle circumferenced the woman's neck. It had perfectly healed into the resemblance of what looked like a choker necklace as it indented into the skin.

"What in the world could have done that?" The other nurse flinched and covered the wound back up with fresh bandages.

"Who knows, The world these days. Did you hear what she was saying? I couldn't quite make it out, but it sounded like Spanish or something." The nurses finished picking up the mess and gathered their things.

"I don't know," The one nurse pulls the woman's hair back out of her face.

"Such a shame. She sure is a pretty little thing. So sad, maybe when she wakes up this time, we can make some since out of this mess. Find out who she is." The nurse secures the woman's hair back behind her and tucks her in one more time before gathering her things.

"Yeah, just let her sleep for a little while till the sedative wears off and I'll call the detective. He's never going to believe she woke up. He leaves those flowers for her once a month. Comes here and checks on her and takes the old flowers and replaces them with new. He's going to be so excited. Go check on Ms. Withers in room 326 and I'll make the call."

The nurses exit the room, and the woman rests peacefully. As you can see her eyes moving back and forth in Rem sleep. She dreams.

"Marie Marie, it's time to go, Your majesty. The court is waiting." A chubby servant sets down a tray of tea and scones next to the most beautiful bed.

The covers soft and fluffed as her majesty rolls over lifting her tea to get that first morning sip.

"Are the children ready Martha? It's such a long ride to the palace." Marie stretches and rises from the puff of blankets and pillows.

"Have you had word from Loui?"

"Yes, your Majesty, Things are very tense at the palace. Your presents have been requested. I'll go gather the children and their things.

The dream skips about in her head.

The carriage, the horses, the sounds of arriving at the palace. The people cry and scream behind the fence as they ride through. The clash of things being thrown at the carriage and the children crying in fear as she holds them tight. Soothing them, reassuring them it's all going to be alright while the servants hide the angry mob in the windows.

Again, she is back at the square, her elegances stripped down to nothing but a simple robe.

She looks down, her hand is in his. As they are both being pushed and pulled through the crowd. The mob, always the mob, the smell of it permeates her senses. The ruggedness of the people and their hatred for their king. And her their Queen, how did it get like this? How could it have led to this. The last moments of her life the stench of blood and the mob. The feel of splintered wood around her neck as she closes her eyes not to see her husband pulled away from her in the same fate. And her children she could hear their screams forced to watch the death of their parents. The death of their country. Her blood pressure spikes, and the machines again go off. The dreams haunt her even in sedation, she dreams.

"Mam.? Mam Are you there?" The Doctor slowly pulls her hand up and brushes it back and forth with his.

Slowly consciousness returns, it's only in bits and pieces, my eyes are so heavy. I can see white all arounds and feel the presences of two men standing next to me.

As my eyes open, I can hear them talking to each other in

English.

"Eau, Verre d'eau." I gasp, the words quiet and unsure.

"What was that mam? The man in the white coat leaned in.

"Water, s'il te plait, Plez. The word slowly came back to me.

"You Speak English I asked as I peered up at the man?

"Yes mam, I'm Doctor Jarreau. We are here at Liberty General Hospital in Washington D.C. What is your Name?"

"Washington D.C.? Where is that?" I sat up slowly. My head still pounding, my words still slow and unsure of what was happening and where I was.

"Washington D.C. mam, do you have any memory of how you got here? A tall handsome man in a suit leaned in. "Take it slow."

"Let's start with your name."

"My name, oh ummm my name..." I feel like I know my name. I think I should know my name."

The room swooned around as I could see things that I didn't recognize. It all seemed so foreign.

"What is this place?" I looked around disoriented.

"It is a hospital, mam?" The man's smile was nice.

"A hospital? Oh, I have been to hospitals before, I think. My name... "

The two men were standing at the end of the bed whispering.

"She seems disoriented still, let's give her some time she's obviously been through a lot, and I need to make my rounds.

"Thank you, Doctor." The doctor exited the room, and the other man came to the side of my bed.

"Hi, do you mind if I sit down." He pushed the blanket to the side and leaned against the side of the bed.

"I'm Detective Gunst. I work here in the D.C. area, in the homicide division."

He leaned over and straightened the flowers on the table.

"I was first on the scene when they found you."

"Do you remember anything at all about who or why this might have happened to you?"

"When, they found me? Like this?"

I reached up and felt the bandages around my neck, the wound was healed but I could still feel the sting of the fragile skin that was now exposed, as I pulled the bandages down.

I glanced around the room, and then back to the man who was seated to my side.

"They found you in the river, I was called due to the circumstances. The wound around your neck was fresh, and no one could identify you. Still, no one has stepped forward with any information at all. Your whole existence is a complete mystery."

He looked me in the eyes, and I still looked around hoping to find some sort of comfort in my surroundings.

"How long have I been here?"

"Six months, we were beginning to think you'd never wake up, if it wasn't for the fact that you had rem dreams, they would have given up on you all together.

And the jewelry of course. "

"Jewelry?" I looked down at my hand. Somehow, I knew I was missing a wedding ring.

"I'm married?"

"Apparently you were wearing some extremely expensive pieces of jewelry. Things people haven't seen in maybe hundreds of years or so. Maybe even priceless."

I searched my mind for something, anything that would make me remember but it was all such a blur.

"Your accent? Are you French?"

He was so kind, and I was so confused about how or why this was all happening.

"I don't know." I looked up at him with tears in my eyes.

"What am I wearing?"

"I feel like I should know something, but it all seems so different so strange."

"Well, Take your time, It's okay. I'm just really glad your awake." He smiled.

"Are you hungry? The nurse walked into the room with a tray of food.

"Oh yes, I'm famished. Tea and scones, oh thank you so much Martha."

"Oh honey, my name is Mary. She laughed and set the tray down on the table and pulled it over my lap.

The detective walked over to the window and was talking into a little thing as the nurse lifted the tray lids.

'What is this? Where is the tea?" I picked at the tray. What strange food this was, I can't remember if I had ever eaten such things.

"Can I eat this?"

Oh, honey I know hospital food isn't the best, but you need your strength. She laughed and exited the room.

"What is this? Is this food?

The detective walked over and laughed as he took off the top of the red Jello container.

"Here try this, it's usually the best thing when it comes to hospital food."

"Is this peasant food? I have seen some things like this, I think.

I wish I had some cake, it's so strange, I am just craving cake."

"Cake huh, maybe we can find you a piece around here somewhere." He laughed and I immediately started to feel better.

I looked up at him and smiled.

"Do you think I will get my memory back."

I sure hope so, I hope we can find the perpetrators that did this to you and bring them to justice.

"Oh, thank you so very much." I smiled and cozied back into the bed.

"Here I have to go for a while, but I'll be back to check on you and see if you remember anything else. Why don't you watch some T.V. and relax for a while."

"T.V.?"

He handed me a strange device that when he pushed the buttons turned on a picture show.

"You think I would remember these things, No?"

"Right." He laughed and out the door he went.

I pushed the buttons and was astonished by what I saw.

I had no recollect of this world I was in. But I watched, I saw many unsettled people.

The feeling of the world stirred inside of me and with civil tensions being scattered through the T.V. I could sense the most awful feelings inside of me. The feeling of dread as if somehow, I had seen this all before. I pushed the button and turned it off. I sat there alone in the room. The feelings of nothing making since or feeling familiar disturbing the feeling of how this TV programs made me feel. As if although I could not remember it was all just happening the same. I flipped over, grabbed the pillow, buried my face into it and began to cry. What was happening. Why couldn't I remember. Did I really want to sleep after an endless slumber.

I sat up and tested to see how else my body worked. I slid my feet onto the floor. The pressure of my weight distributed. I could hold myself up, but I was very weak. I made my way to what looked like the bathroom where I felt around, until I felt a switch.

Popping the switch up, I saw myself standing in the doorway. My reflection in the mirror. My long wild hair had been pulled back out of my face and the bandages were pulled down exposing the bright pink scar. I felt the scar as I looked at it. Running my fingers across the ridges of tender skin. I stood there for a while, just looking at myself, trying to remember who I was and how I got here and if any of this was real. My body is smooth and pale. This whole world is foreign and strange. The gown full of snaps that covered the tubes that still ran into bags of what seemed to be water. I'm dizzy and overwhelmed, so I make my way back to the bed where I look for the servant's bell. Where is the bell. No matter, I guess. I lay down and soon I drifted to sleep.

Mademoiselle, mademoiselle, your dresses have arrived. Come, it's time for your bath.

I drifted back into reality as a nurse stood there holding a dress made of flowered fabric.

"I found this in the goodwill and thought it would look good on you. Come now, I think it's your size. Detective Gunst will be here soon, and I think he's going to take you to the station if you're up for it.

The doctor said as long as you're feeling okay and all."

She was excited and happy to see me feeling better these days, I could tell.

"It's going to be okay." She slipped the hospital gown over my head and placed the dress back in its place.

"Come on child get up and look at yourself." She scurried me out of the bed and I stood there looking at myself again in the mirror. The dress was simple, but I felt pretty, as I turned myself around. "

"But what about..." I barely got the words out of my mouth when she turned around and smiled at me.

"I thought about that too." She pulled a pretty pink scarf out of the bag and slipped it over my head and then tied it around my neck. I smiled and hugged her tight. She was the only person I had really talked to since I woke up and she had treated me with the upmost kindness a person in my position could ask for.

She was finishing the bow just as detective --- walked in.

"Well, well you look gorgeous." He looked down at the floor as he spoke.

I curtseyed. Grabbing the folds of the simple flowered dress, that somehow made me feel so much better.

"Are you ready my dear, I sure hope you're up for this. I know it's going to be hard, but I'll be there with you the whole time." He gently placed his arm in mine, and we made our way down the hall. I had been able to look out the windows but that's as far as I had been able to go until today, so the butterflies swooned in my stomach as I entered what they all called an elevator. I giggled as I felt the room move beneath my feet and he smiled as I fell back and grabbed ahold of the walls.

"You know this is going to be really hard, we haven't talked much about police stations and what goes on in them. They will have a lot of pictures of how they found you and well what you were wearing and such."

"I know," I looked down at the floor. My shoes were a little too big and I thought they didn't match the dress very well.

"But maybe going through this will make me remember who I am. Then maybe you can call me by my name instead of yes dear." I laughed as the elevator door opened and the sights and sounds of the bustling city came into full effect.

As I looked around all my senses came alive. The bright light of the sun and the heat of the day hit me while the loud screeches of the cars and the people filled my ears. The detective grabbed my arm and pulled me out of the way as a man on a bicycle raced past me. The amazement of the world around me apparent, as he hurried me into his car and started it up.

"I feel like I should know something about the world by now it's been two weeks since I woke up and it all just seems so strange still to me. I'm really sorry everything is so hard on me."

I looked over at him, he was looking around trying to see everything around him.

"I've learned a lot from the TV." I was trying to be as pleasant as possible.

The sights were amazing as we cruised down the busy streets.

"Hey, did you see that? It was a horse. I saw a horse and buggy just over there. I think I love horses".

I wrestled with the belt holding me in place.

"Wait can we turn around."

The familiar feeling of that buggy made me feel good and I wanted to see it again.

"Deary, we can't see the horses right now. We have to get to the station. There are people there that are waiting for us." He was firm in his voice as he cruised in and out of the cars around him.

We finally reached a tall building that was appealing in architecture to me. The tall white columns seemed nice and the seal above the door reminiscent to my mind.

"Is this the place?"

"Yeah, I have to park and then we can go in. Are you ready?" He looked at me with some sadness. I knew this was going to be tough, but I had to have hope that maybe something would make me remember.

I sat there as he got out of the car and waited for him to open my door. He looked at me through the glass and then ran over to my side of the car. "

Okay your highness lets go." He grabbed my hand and helped me out of the car. I stood there looking up at the tall building as if this was going to be the day, I received the answers I needed to start my life.

Looking into his eyes, I took my first step up the stairs.

As we walked into the building the hallway was bustling with men and women in uniforms all reminiscent of the familiar course of an army or guards that seemed to bring comfort yet insight nervous fears with in me.

The detective ushered me hastily past the crowds into a small room where a small group of individuals sat at a table.

"Is she ready for this?" A woman looked at Detective Gunst, and then rolled her eyes at me as I sat into the chair and fidgeted about trying to calm myself.

"She is as ready as she is ever going to be." He nodded at the lady and took the seat next to me.

"Mam, I know this is going to be shocking and hard for you but if we are ever going to solve the mystery of what happened to you, we must show you the circumstances of how we found you and see if it jogs your memory at all.

The lady was stern but kind, so I nodded my head as to allow her to begin.

A small device sat next to her and as she flipped the switch on it, she began to speak.

"Today is July 3rd, 2023, we are recording these proceedings in hope to reassemble the memory in the victim which is suffering from memory lose as to the crimes that happened on the night of February 20th, 2023, in which the victim was found floating in the Potomac River near the old town docks."

The female officer kept speaking but as she spoke the room began to spin and a nervousness that came over me forced images into my mind.

"The door! They are at the door." The voices of the past swooned through the air as the people at the table looked at me.

"Deary are you alright?"

Detective Gunst put his hand on my arm.

"Take your time, just breathe." He looked into my eyes, but the voices kept coming and I sat there frozen in fear as the women took the pictures out and laid them in front of me.

The images were horrific. A young woman, me, waterlogged in a long gown being pulled from the river. The long gown was covered in blood as if she had been drenched by a bucket of blood thrown over her head. Fading down into what seemed to be at one time a white dress.

"Are you okay" The detectives spoke. I could hear the words, but the sounds of the mob started to echo through my head like a tornado.

The alarm shook my body and I felt myself losing control of my sanity as I jumped out of the chair and hid myself in the corner.

The detective rushed over to comfort me but all I could hear was the crowds screaming and the images of them pulling us. My husband Loui was in front of me.

The fear consumed by body while the people in the room thought they were helping calm me, but the intense memories permeated my mind. As I shrunk myself into a ball on the floor. The hands of the detectives, the hands of the mob pulling me up to my fate.

Suddenly it came to me I knew in that moment what and why I was here. I pushed the people off of me with my might, they were panicking all the while trying to help calm me. But the voices were too loud, and I had to make them listen, I had to make them see.

As I sat there in my panic reliving the memories, I saw Detective Gunst. He was trying to talk to get me to come back from the fear.

"Listen to my voice." He cried. "I'm here with you. You are safe." Follow my voice back. What are you seeing?"

The fear trembled inside of me. I could hear my mind telling me what had to be done. I began to find my voice and to scream.

"The answer, I know what I have to do."

"What is it Deary, what is it."

A loud scream came from deep within me as if it wasn't even me, but I knew it was the truth."

"WWEEEEEE we,

No,

I,

I have to...

I must feed the People." The screams bellowed from deep within me.

"I HAVE TO FEED THE PEOPLE."

I FEEL THE ROOM SPIN ONE MORE TIME AND I WAS GONE.

Made in the USA
Columbia, SC
12 May 2025

57850107R00248